UPON THE RIVEN THRONE

MELISSA WRIGHT

Cover design and illustration by Ireen Chau

Interior illustrations by

Ireen Chau https://www.ireenchau.com

Grace Crandall @krasnetigritsa

Teresa Vu https://www.peachiemochi.com

Marta García Navarro @margana_mgn

Myrthena @myrthena

UPON THE RIVEN THRONE

Once upon a time, in a not terribly far-off kingdom, there lived a king and his daughter who had been so fortunate in all their undertakings that the kingdom was enormously rich. The king and his daughter had everything they fancied and did not find their lives bore much burden at all. But the king stood against an unjust foe—an evil fae queen intent on stealing the kingdom—and soon misfortune befell him, one ill lot after another. And all the splendid furniture, books, and precious goods could not save the kingdom from danger. The king had suddenly lost every-thing by dint of accident, illness, and disaster. His courtiers betrayed him. His wheat stores turned foul.

The princess tried to stand brave and cheerful in the face of such wretchedness. But both she and the king knew it was not simply a run of bad luck. The evil queen was gathering power. With every kingdom she conquered, their defenses dashed like ships in a storm-tossed sea, her magic grew. Norcliffe was meant to be her next accession, and it was clear Princess Mireille specifically had become her prey. Norcliffe could not be protected by might alone and the king loved his daughter dearly, but the evil queen had to be stopped. Soon she would grow too powerful to be beaten.

When a fae queen was trying to have one murdered, it was usually quick work. So nothing was left for the princess but to take her departure with haste, to escape to a place outside the neighboring kingdom of Westrende where the secrets of fae magic were rooted deep. As the servants could no longer be trusted, she'd brought only her childhood friend Thomas, known to the kingdom as Lord Holden, skilled historian and seasoned bachelor.

One might think that a woman of such desperate fortune must be in want of a well-positioned ally, or at least of refuge. One would be right. But sometimes all that was available was an adversary in the form of a husband. Which was why Princess Mireille of Norcliffe stood in the midst of a dark forest that seemed to be the most dismal place on the face of the earth.

"Are you certain you'd not rather flee to the sea?" Thomas asked from beside her.

Mireille's chuckle was grim. "Would that we could, Thomas. Would that we could."

Before them rose a facade of the wall that marked the Rive—the ancient boundary separating the human kingdom of Westrende from the land of the fae. Beneath its carved stone glamour rested a skeleton of fine filigree metal, iron to be precise, binding the magic of the wilds and meant to keep conflict at bay. The marshal of Westrende stood at the edge of the trees with a company of kingsmen, all watching from a distance to ensure Mireille's safety—at least until she'd made it across.

Law prevented Westrende officials from going any farther, and though the council governing the kingdom was firmly against anything fae, they could not stop Mireille. She was first and foremost a princess of Norcliffe, after all. They had no say in the deal she was about to strike, despite that the fae prince wanted nothing more than to destroy the wall and Westrende's safety, and held kingdom officials ransom in his fight to do so.

The fae had been trapped within the boundary for so long that citizens of Westrende had begun to believe their existence nothing more than tales, that the warnings to never speak their name were only superstition. But the kingdom officials did not want to stop Mireille, not entirely, because the threat of the fae queen was much more dangerous than any human kingdom could face alone.

Which meant an empire of fae kingdoms was the only thing they could fathom that might be worse than the fae lands the princess was about to step into.

Mireille glanced at Thomas. "What about you? Last chance to sprint for freedom. I would not begrudge you any attempt at escape."

His smile was wry. "You'll not be rid of me so easily, Highness. You know how I adore adventure."

Thomas did not adore adventure. But he was loyal, and Mireille knew he wasn't about to let her walk into this mess alone. She turned to face him, brushing a hand over the skirt of her traveling gown. "Very well, no sense in putting it off any longer. How do I look?"

"As if you've trekked through a sinister forest. What about me?"

"As if you could slay a flock of maidens with just a wink."

"That bad?" He frowned. "A lord does generally wish to win hearts without bothering to make eye contact first."

She lifted a shoulder. "They're maidens of very high willpower. I don't make the rules."

Thomas watched her patiently. In truth, the man had always won hearts with less than a glance. He was handsome, fair-haired, square-jawed, and finely dressed, with the sort of smile that felt at once intimate and playful. To Mireille, he had been both courtier and confidant. He was her truest friend, and he knew her well enough to guess that she was delaying.

He tapped the hilt of his sword. "Would you like me to say it for you? I've never called on a fae prince before. It would be a novelty to summon one. You know how I adore novelty."

Thomas did not adore novelty. Mireille flexed her hands and shook out her fingers, then moved to stand beside him. She was about to seal her bargain with a fae—creatures so powerful, so dangerous, that the ancients had long ago built a wall to keep their kind in. She'd be a fool for what she was doing, if not for the *not doing it* being a greater danger still.

She drew her shoulders back and spoke the true name of the fae prince of Rivenwilde. The magic that constrained the prince would force his appearance, but he was not its instrument. He would twist the situation to his advantage. Mireille had no intention of letting him use her for anything besides overcoming the fae queen.

He was there in an instant, stealing into view as if shifting from shadow, donned in black from head to toe, expression cold and magic prickling awareness over Mireille's skin. The tines of his crown rose majestic and feral, his dress impeccable right down to the embroidered waistcoat and finely tied cravat. Too late for Mireille to swallow the words back and flee, she stood firm beneath his scrutiny.

The prince could not possibly be unaware of the kingsmen watching, given the way his jaw ticked, but he pointedly did not look toward their spot near the trees. He had known Mireille was coming, and that was all that truly mattered. He straightened to an impressive height, then dipped into a generous bow. "Your Highness."

"Mireille," she said automatically.

His dark eyes lifted, staying on hers as he rose. His voice

was rich and steady, and, most unsettlingly, the forest around them seemed to hold its breath. "Mireille."

She waited for him to return the courtesy, allowing her expectation of it to stand plainly between them.

The edge of his mouth seemed tempted to frown, but evidently he was not above caving to societal pressure. "You may call me Alder."

It was a small win but she would take it. "May I introduce Lord Holden?"

The prince inclined his head, and Thomas said, "Thomas, please."

Thomas only received a brusque nod, no invitation to familiarity.

Prince Alder returned his attention to Mireille. It felt like a great deal of attention, given that he was only one man, but she remained steady. Their agreement had already been settled—Mireille would never have made the trek to the greenwood otherwise—but he evidently thought she needed a reminder of the terms before the bargain was officially sealed, because he said, "Once you cross the boundary, you will be tied by bargain. You will not be released. You will not be allowed to return home."

"I understand."

He was incredibly tall, his dark hair confined by the crown of tangled bone-like spikes. There was a lean elegance about him and despite the crispness of his manner, he did not seem entirely discourteous. He held himself like that of a person of immense power. But there were many kinds of power, and his was the sort that could fell the surrounding trees with the flick of a wrist. An entire kingdom of fae were beneath his rule. Mireille understood that and more.

He said, "If you come at all, you must come willingly."

"I do come willingly." A strange sensation of magic seemed to shift in the soil beneath her feet. She did not look away from the prince, though, in truth, Mireille's willingness was dependent on circumstance. She would not be so inclined without sufficient duress in the form of one very unpleasant fae queen. But the threats to her life and kingdom were more than sufficient, so the words had not been a lie. Even if she had not told the prince of her reasoning.

The prince's attention never wavered. "You will be given one month at my palace under the laws of hospitality. By the next moon, if you mean to stay under my protection, it will be as my bride."

"And if I do not? What then?" What if she did not say the vows that would bind them by law. What if she did not uphold her word.

Bearing unchanged, he said, "Those who have offered themselves under bargain may not be released."

Thomas leaned forward to put in, "Unless they pay the price to break that bargain before time is up."

His statement was roundly ignored. Near the trees, one of the Westrende kingsmen coughed.

For Mireille's part, she had not even asked the price to break their bargain. The due for bargain-breaking was always more than a person could satisfy, and never a matter of petty wealth but one of unthinkable sacrifice. Whatever it was, she would not be able to pay it. The fae did not allow humans into their realm only to let them return to their homeland freely. She asked, "What happens if we are not wed at the turn of the moon? I will no longer be protected by the laws of hospitality. I will not be treated as a guest. But should I go through with the marriage or not..."

The prince's manner seemed to darken. A chill breeze swept the clearing. He said, "Either way, you will belong to me."

His queen or as his captive, that was her choice. Mireille wet her lips. She'd heard many tales regarding how prisoners of the fae were kept. She would be deciding between that uncertain fate or becoming a member of the Riven Court. It may have seemed like an obvious course, but the fae court held dangers of its own. Dangers that might make a person beg for the discomforts of a small, dark cell. And should she marry the prince of Rivenwilde, she could no longer be heir to Norcliffe, not when the entire reason she left was to keep it safe from the fae.

Neither situation would be as unpleasant as the fate that awaited her outside of his protection, though. If she did not find a way to defeat the queen, Norcliffe and everyone Mireille loved would be destroyed. The month she'd been gifted as his guest needed to be enough. Whether she was confined by walls or by vows, Mireille had to get close enough to the prince to discover the secrets of fae magic, but not close enough to risk him discovering her own.

She gave a quick, decisive nod. "I accept your terms. Let us away."

The prince's gaze held a hint of wariness as it flicked toward Thomas, then returned to lock on Mireille's. "Very well." Mireille thought it telling that he would have suspicion of the agreement at all, but he said, "It is agreed." The power beneath her feet swelled, and the prince, the clearing, and Mireille's future all seemed to shift by unknowable degrees.

It was done. Her fate was sealed. Mireille moved to take the prince's arm, and there was a moment of awareness between them that he had not yet offered. More hesitation, it seemed, despite that their bargain was settled. It was a solid reminder that the arrangement was bigger than just the two of them. Mireille gave a farewell glance toward the Westrende marshal, who returned a firm nod. It was unclear whether Westrende had any faith she might succeed.

Head inclined slightly, the prince finally lifted his arm,

Mireille slid her hand through, and they walked together toward the wall.

"Thomas," she reminded the prince.

He blinked at her, then, evidently understanding, cleared his throat. "One does not have to be touching a fae to pass through once the gateway is open."

"Oh." She did not let go. "Well, at least, do not forget him."

Behind them, Thomas muffled a chuckle. He was carrying a single small bag, the entirety of both their possessions since their departure from Norcliffe had been executed with as much stealth as possible, and he was the only bit of security and sense of home that Mireille had left. It was calming to hear the hint of levity from him and to know that her friend was at her back.

The prince's jaw flexed but not, it seemed, with shared humor. He did not seem to be having a great deal of fun stealing away a human princess under the watchful gaze of his sworn Westrende enemies, truth be told. But before another breath, they were walking through the wall, its filigree wires uncurling to surround and gather the prince, its magic parting in a manner that Mireille was not quite able to make sense of, even as she was drawn inside the boundary with him. She could see through the wall's glamour to the cage beneath and feel the magic around her, in a way that felt as if it could not be denied, no matter how much power one might possess. It was an insistent pressure not only against her skin but every part of her being, as if gravity, like diving from the cliffs of her home into the icy waters of the sea. Not that a princess would do such a thing. But if she had—very similar.

They came through the other side and the prince pointedly did not glance at her, heaving in breath and clinging to his arm as she was, or at Thomas, who Mireille was grateful to find had made it through and was again at her side. Thomas was a little green and looked as if he might be regretting not taking that last chance to flee but when he met her gaze, he gave a halfhearted nod.

They had made it.

Through the wall, only. The easiest step. Mireille wasn't even certain it counted as a step in her plans. She should have made a list so that she might check off *getting to the forest* and *finding the wall*, lest that was all they would manage. It was always good to feel accomplished.

"Shall we pause for a moment?"

The prince's words brought a huff of helpless laughter from Mireille's chest. "No," she said finally. "That was quite an experience, but I believe Thomas and I have our land legs once more. Do carry on."

His brow pinched. "I thought it best to walk through our domain but that was inconsiderate after the journey you've already made. I shall bring us closer at once."

Mireille opened her mouth to protest but before a word was out, the three of them were transported to a different path entirely. The objection died in her throat. They stood suddenly between an avenue of trees, leaves overhead shifting in the warm afternoon breeze and laying patchy shade over the path. The avenue ended at a splendid palace, but she could not take her eyes off the canopy, made up of orange trees and covered with flowers and fruit.

The prince seemed to notice her gaping, so she explained, "I've only ever seen them in illustrations."

He paused, his gaze flicking between her eyes with something that was not quite so distant before he released her from his arm. He crossed to a low branch at the edge of the path then reached up, and his long, graceful fingers pinched off one of the delicate blossoms. When he returned to offer it to Mireille, their bare skin brushed, and she felt a flutter of his magic once more.

She turned the blossom in her fingers before lifting it to her nose. It smelled sweet and bright over a hint of something bitter, with a trace of other, more familiar fragrances. She quite liked it.

The prince was watching her from where he stood, rather close, Thomas unmistakably looking away from them both.

Mireille tucked the blossom into the collar of her jacket then glanced up at the prince. "Thank you."

His eyes held a strange hint of warmth in the dappled light as they rose from the blossom to trail over her face, the stillness in his form giving Mireille the impression that he was uncertain how to respond. She took hold of his arm once more so that he didn't have to.

The three approached the palace under the distrustful gazes of onlookers who appeared to consist of palace staff and members of court, all of them fae. Mireille held her chin high, eyes forward, and wished she'd chosen a slightly richer gown. She had been unsure what to expect but the opulence of the fae court was impressive, even to one who'd seen a fair share of fine and fancy places.

The lawn was lovely, lush with greenery and blooming flowers, alive with birdsong, and formed in such a way as to create a natural path toward the agate steps leading to the imposing palace. In the distance, trees rose impossibly high, their boughs no doubt obscuring the many dwellings of Rivenwilde's fae. Mireille could not be certain of what lay beyond, though, because illustrations of the kingdom had not been available to anyone outside the wall, and what few sketches Thomas had been able to find were clearly only those of fancy. Fae were secretive, and Rivenwilde fae most of all.

As they reached the top of the steps, the prince's chest rose in a deep breath, and the sensation of magic seemed to rise with it, like the swell of the sea. His gaze stayed forward as they strode through the door, his arm steady beneath hers.

A massive archway opened into the entrance hall, where they were met by a smartly dressed fae man who appeared to be near the prince's age. His skin was the same dark olive as Mireille's, but where her hair was long and light chestnut, his was in short, neat waves of dark mahogany.

"Mireille," the prince said, as if it pained him to speak her name so casually, "may I introduce Noal?"

The man fell into a deep bow.

"Noal will be at your service for any need. You will have all the food and care you want for, at any hour."

"Because of the laws of hospitality," Mireille said.

The prince's jaw flexed. Again, not with humor. "Not because you are a guest of the prince of Rivenwilde. Because you are his betrothed."

She met his gaze. Mireille might not be able to find maps of Rivenwilde, but she knew the laws of hospitality would protect his guests, and until she was thrown into a fae prison for breaking their agreement or thrown into the fae court once she'd followed through, she possessed a title that was equal to his own. A princess would require the highest of care or he would be breaking one of the oldest fae tenets.

He said, "You are under my protection."

"And what of Thomas?" Mireille asked.

"My protection extends to Lord Holden as well." The prince's voice was level. "While you are both within these walls."

"So if we were to leave…"

"Do not leave these walls."

The words felt sharper than Mireille might have expected, and she glanced at Noal to determine if the man seemed to think the reaction out of the ordinary. Noal, however, was staring wide-eyed at the orange blossom tucked into the collar of Mireille's jacket. His gaze slid accusingly toward the prince.

An unspoken message passed between Noal and his sovereign.

"What's this?" Thomas said, edging closer as he gestured between the two. "What's happening there?"

"I do not know what you mean," Noal said, just as the prince said, "Nothing."

The prince did not flick an annoyed glance at his man, but it was clear he wished to. He said, "I must take my leave now."

Mireille asked, "Why?"

The prince froze mid-bow. "I must attend to..."

She suspected he might have been about to answer something like *important prince concerns* when his words dried up.

Instead, he said, "I should allow you to get settled in. You have had a long journey."

She glanced down at her gown, the hem damp and stuck with briars. "Yes, I suppose that's so. I shall dress for our first dinner together, and resume your company then."

When she glanced back up, he was already halfway to the door. He stopped at her words. A moment later, he turned back to face her. "Dinner?"

"We must have dinner together."

"I am... Quite a bit occupies my time."

"Very busy," Noal added helpfully. "Barely an hour free for meals."

The prince shot him a look that promised violence.

"You must have dinner with me," Mireille said. "Every night."

He stared at her, aghast.

"I've only a month to come to know you, to understand what becoming a part of your world will mean." A mere month to uncover his secrets, to safeguard Norcliffe by whatever means necessary to prevent the villainous... villainess from folding it into her malevolent empire. "If you prefer, I could accompany you with whatever you're about. It would be no trouble at all, as I'm to be idle here every moment of every day, unable to leave the palace and unable to plan visits from my friends. A guest must be entertained, after all."

His eyes narrowed infinitesimally. Mireille gave him her most winsome smile. "Alder," she started, and something seemed to roll through him at the word.

He held up a hand, as if to forestall her speaking it again. "Dinner. When it is feasible."

"Every night."

Thomas and Noal stood rapt, no attempt at hiding the looks they were darting between their prince and princess.

The prince's mouth shifted, leaving no doubt he understood her challenge. "As you wish, Mireille. We will dine together, every night. Until the turn of the moon."

CHAPTER 2

Mireille and Thomas were led to their rooms, Mireille's lovely and spacious with his smaller suite adjoining hers. Had she any doubt about the faithfulness of the prince to the laws of hospitality, they would have been thoroughly quashed. Even their wardrobes and chests had been filled with the finest garments, fine gowns for her and a variety of jackets for Thomas. She had a full sitting room, a sewing room, a bathing chamber, and a bed so wide she'd be hard pressed to find the edge of it when she woke in the dark.

There was one other door, which Noal discreetly explained could only be opened by magic, and never would, for it belonged to the prince. Essentials covered, Noal said, "I trust all is to your satisfaction. Should you find yourself wanting, you are only to call."

"I am most appreciative. Thomas and I will try not to be much of a bother," Mireille said.

Noal inclined his head. "After you've rested, I would be pleased to take you on a tour of the palace."

"No." She pressed her lips. "Of course it is generous of you to offer, but I would prefer to be shown by the prince."

"The prince is—"

"Very busy, I know." Her finger slid over the gilt edge of a fine porcelain bowl. "Perhaps while the prince and I are occupied at dinner you could show Thomas the grounds. He will certainly want to find the lay of the land."

Perhaps the pair of them could be kept busy while Mireille tried to make headway with the prince. Perhaps Thomas could gain information from the staff that Mireille could not from their sovereign. Thomas was, after all, an expert in securing delicate—and concealed—information. Despite that he betrayed not a tap of the finger, he was surely itching to discover as much as possible as soon as possible about the palace they'd found their way into.

"As you wish," said Noal. "I will leave you to prepare for dinner."

The moment the man was gone, Thomas and Mireille scoured the room, searching for any traps or trickery, checking beneath the bedclothes, testing the door locks, and peering beneath the rugs.

"I don't see anything," Mireille said, cheek pressed to the plaster as she gave a one-eyed survey of the wall behind a painting. "What if he doesn't want to trick us at all? What if the prince truly is committed to their rules about guests?"

"Alder," Thomas reminded her. "You need to get used to calling him by his name. You know the fae cannot tolerate that sort of thing. Did you see him all but twitch when you said it in the hall?"

It was true. But it was not the magic she had used in the forest. Summoning a prince by name only worked outside of his palace. While she was a guest in his home, she could not expect more than what hospitality required. He would not simply materialize with a word. He was not at her beck and call. "I think he hates it when I say his name."

Thomas chuckled darkly where he was bent over examining the underside of a settee. "I think he does not know what to make of you. And what was with that look that passed between the pair of them regarding the orange blossom?"

Mireille shrugged. "Perhaps it was considered a gift? I know much less about fae traditions than I would like. We will have to find the library soon."

"Before we unintentionally break any laws, you mean."

"Unintentional or not, I prefer to be prepared. See if Noal will show you the dungeon."

He glanced up at her from where he inspected the bowl of fruit resting on the small table near the settee. "You think there's a dungeon beneath the palace?"

"Or cells, at least. It would keep the prince from having to set protections against his secrets. Should the prisoners be released, the laws of hospitality would prevent them from speaking of what they witnessed while under his roof."

Thomas held her gaze. "Prisoners of the fae are not released."

"On occasion. In exchange for someone else, sometimes." Her lips drew down. "It happens."

He shifted his weight to one leg, the lordly equivalent of a disapproving finger-wag. "And a dungeon is not exactly hospitable."

"There's food and a bed. It counts. We both know we're only in a suite because of my station. We are fortunate he's not decided to twist the terms in order to stick us somewhere less pleasant, traps or no." She shook out her hands. "Regardless. We're here now and there doesn't seem to be any immediate risk. Best prepare for dinner. Who knows what time the fae eat meals?"

"Right. You get a bath and I'll lay out your dress."

"You? Pick my wardrobe?"

His nose scrunched. "Are you truly questioning whether I'm the right person for the task? That I would not know the best gown to display a woman's figure?"

"Not my figure."

He rolled his eyes. "I'm your friend, not your brother."

"Thomas!"

"What? I've noticed. As has every other lord who's attended a ball with you, even if their attention is only surreptitious. Trust that I know which gowns brought out the most lecherous leers."

"You think the prince a lecher?"

"Not at all. But I think him a man. I think he has eyes. We will use every tool we might to your advantage."

She crossed her arms. "This may be the single most offensive conversation we've had, Thomas. I think you should know that."

"Highness, if this conversation offends you, you're in no way prepared for fae court." He glanced back at her after he opened the wardrobe door. "Or the cut of their gowns."

THOMAS HAD BEEN RIGHT, Mireille was not prepared for the cut of the provided gown. Deep, shimmering blue with a low-cut square bodice and a thin, slim fitting skirt, the gown left little to the imagination. Worse, Thomas had draped her in jewels, making certain that the candlelight would catch on the bare skin above the gown. She'd been given no gloves, no shawl, and no sense of how, exactly, their dinner was meant to go.

When Noal arrived to her suite, he only gave a vague gesture of approval before conducting her from the room.

A few fae moved silently past them, with no more than the whisper of cloth trailing behind. Noal took Mireille through many long corridors, each so unlike the ones she'd grown up surrounded by in her castle home. Instead of tapestry and portraiture over block, the palace walls were as smooth as polished marble, featuring carved scenes that seemed as alive as the vines that grew at every corner and column. It was nonsensical, as if a courtyard garden had been brought indoors. Mireille adored it.

A dozen questions populated in her mind, impatient for the moment it would be socially acceptable for her to pester Noal for information. His pace slowed as he led her past a music room, then he paused before a pair of finely carved doors, not quite near enough to imply he meant to open them.

Through the narrow gap between wood and stone, the prince's voice carried. It was muffled, but his tone was plainly angry, his words clipped. "...I will not be told how to manage my own affairs."

A feminine voice replied, the sound smooth with fury, though Mireille could not quite make out the words. Clear enough was that it was an argument.

Mireille was no fool. Eavesdropping on royalty was a trespass she was not about to commit in front of a witness. She moved to tug her arm free of Noal's but he stepped forward, as if he'd only paused to release her and open the doors all along. She wasn't fooled by that, either.

At the sound of Noal's entry, the heated confrontation inside the room broke off. Noal released the lever, drawing himself straight as his gloved hands crossed at the wrists. "Her Highness, Princess Mireille," he said.

Mireille stepped forward and the room's two occupants

snapped their focus to her. The prince stood near a tall woman with warm skin and bright, tipped-up eyes. She wore a fine silk gown with sleeves to the knuckle and an embroidered train, but there appeared to be several broken twigs stuck through the fabric of the hem. The woman stared at Mireille in an introspective sort of way, while the prince's eyes were narrowed menacingly. It was not entirely surprising that the prince's gaze revealed displeasure, given that he'd done so from the start, but the way it aimed at first her, then Noal in a more accusatory way, did not bode well for the night's event.

Alder crossed the room, his suit no less black than the one in which she'd first encountered him, but certainly more formal. Noal remained steady, shoulders back and hands crossed precisely in the manner of a member of staff, not a hint of the man who'd been impertinent within Mireille's earshot a half dozen times so far.

The prince ended his approach just in front of Mireille and when he leaned forward, taking her hand to bow low over it, she caught the faint scent of bergamot and something more warm and musky. Her hand was bare, as was much of her arm and chest.

His gaze rose. "Highness. So generous of you to grace us with your company."

Though custom demanded no deference, Mireille returned his gesture with a small curtsy. The prince kept hold of her hand, placing it on his arm to lead her farther into the room. He paused before the woman he'd been speaking with. "My sister."

Mireille inclined her head. The woman's lips pursed. Her dark hair was braided through with a delicate jeweled band and, perhaps not intentionally, a thick thorny leaf.

"Nisha is the spare," the prince explained. "You'll find she attends every gathering to protect the throne by preventing threats against my person." There was a brief pause before he added meaningfully, "Lest she have to take my place."

Nisha's mouth twisted in a wry smile as she held his gaze, some unspoken message passing between them, and then the woman glanced purposefully at Mireille, seeming to note her bare hand where it was tucked into Alder's arm. "And what of this one? Does she have claws? Is she a threat against your person?"

The prince gave his sister a quelling look. "*This one,* as you so ineloquently put, is under my protection. You will leave her alone."

He drew his arm—and Mireille's hand with it—closer to his side, then led her from the room. Nisha chuckled as she followed behind them.

When the prince and Mireille stepped through a wide set of doors to the chamber outside the dining hall, two dozen pairs of eyes turned toward them. Fae courtiers stood in their finery, jewels tucked into neatly tied tresses, delicate embroidery trimming dinner jackets, and boots polished to within an inch of their lives. They had clearly been waiting on their prince and, perhaps, on Mireille.

Mireille had no way of knowing to whom the prince had revealed their betrothal, but the gathered fae certainly did not disguise their interest in the pair, paying particular notice to her hand where it was tucked against his arm.

As they walked past the other attendees, the prince not sparing the crowd a glance, Mireille realized none of the others present were wearing a gown cut in the style of her own. In fact, the woman standing nearest wore a garment with extravagant lace shaped so high on the neck that it tipped into a point near her slender ears. Another had a bare throat but full-length gloves and a fur-trimmed drape. The styles were not entirely dissimilar to other royal functions

Mireille had attended, but while her wardrobe cabinet had been stocked with sheer gowns and daring cuts, the fae were dressed in sturdier fabrics trimmed with designs resembling vines and branches, their appeal the fine make, not the figure beneath. They seemed not to judge her for it, but as she'd yet to see another human in the palace or on its grounds, they may have simply been distracted by her appearance at all.

The gathered fae stared on, but the prince moved past the lot of them without introduction.

Dinner with the prince, it turned out, was not the private affair Mireille had anticipated. The dining hall was large and elegant, candelabra lining the walls and dozens of serving staff standing in attendance. At the foot of the table, a tall man uniformed in black drew out a finely carved chair, and as Mireille sat, her fingers slid from the prince's arm. He crossed to the opposite end of the exceedingly long table, past an array of fine dishes, and took his seat in an even grander chair at the table's head. The others came in, filling the long row of seats at either side. Nisha settled two chairs down from the prince, and began conversation with a tall, thin man at her side. Nisha did not particularly favor the prince, but Mireille understood that succession in the fae court was not a mirror of her own court. In fact, she suspected very little of their respective traditions overlapped. She would need to remember that.

The service began without a pause or address, indicating a level of informality. To Mireille's right sat a petite fae with copper hair. When the server leaned forward to place a dish of roast vegetables, a comment passed that caused a smile to split the woman's face and drew a quiet chuckle from the man beside her. To Mireille's left, a stout man with dark hair and deep-set eyes poured amber liquid into Mireille's glass, then gave her a friendly nod while the couple beyond him took candied fruit from a long platter. Aside from their unnatural elegance and grace, and the occasional tell of their magic or strength, the fae around her appeared much like any other royal court. But nothing could have been further from the truth.

A bit of dread swam in Mireille's stomach. She had hoped to meet the prince alone. She was not prepared for whatever rules of propriety his court held, even if the dinner did seem less formal. Her gaze lifted to the opposite end of the table, past serving dishes and ornate candelabra, where the prince leaned forward, his head inclined toward a stately, silver-haired woman to his right but his eyes on Mireille. In the high-backed chair among the group of courtiers, it would not take a crown to recognize who held rule. But the crown was there, a stark reminder of just what Mireille had gotten herself into.

She was too deeply in the situation to do anything but see herself through. She lifted her glass toward the prince, then took a cautious sip of a sweet, fruity cordial. His gaze tracked the motion, staying on her until a server leaned forward and blocked him from view.

"Have you toured the gardens?"

The voice of the man at Mireille's side snapped her attention back to her immediate surroundings. She pasted on a pleasant expression. "I have not. We only just arrived this afternoon. Do you recommend them?"

"Without reservation. The lilies alone…" He sighed wistfully. "Would you agree to let me show them to you? It would only require a bit of your time."

"That sounds lovely—"

Mireille's words cut off as a server leaned between the pair to place a dish of pears onto the table, more heavily than required and before the first course was up. The server's dark eyes met hers. She was thin with short, smooth hair and a chin that came to a delicate point. Her expression remained neutral but the act had clearly been a warning.

When the server drew away, the man asked, "It is agreed then?"

"No. As I was saying, that sounds lovely but I must decline."

"Must you?"

Mireille's fingers tightened around the stem of her glass. "It would be foolish, would it not, to agree to any bargain—no matter how trivial—so readily?"

His answering grin was wide and sharp. When he raised his glass, the gesture seemed intended more toward the server and the interruption than toward Mireille. *Right*, she thought. The games hadn't taken long to commence. Her every step would have to remain measured and cautious. For an entire month, regardless of whatever came after, she could be nothing but vigilant. Bargains were dangerous things. It was impossible to guess what the man's offer might have brought —perhaps Mireille would have awoken to the darkness to find herself helplessly striding toward a nighttime rendezvous. Perhaps something worse. It was difficult to know when even the mention of her time could translate to literal days of her life, or her freedom.

Those were things Mireille did not have to spare.

Conversation carried on around her, no further bargains offered but no real interest from the fae placed near her. They spoke to one another about trivial matters, laughing and nattering without bothering to include their guest, which implied Mireille was only truly considered a guest by the prince and his staff. She took another sip of cordial, the entire ordeal seeming to sour her stomach. If the evenings that followed were much the same, she would never get near the prince, and never discover what she needed.

His eyes met hers once more from across the long table,

and she could swear they mocked her demand for nightly dinners. Another point for him, another chance at answers lost for her. It was not as if she didn't know the fae could not be trusted, but she desperately needed to win. She had known it would not be easy, that the fae loved toying with humans, and that she would be in danger every step of the way. But if she could not outwit a mere prince, what chance did she have with a queen? Mireille let her gaze slide down the row of fae at each side of the table, careful not to linger long on the details she cataloged. Colors, flowers, symbols, and trim. Who preferred jewels, who had jagged nails, whose garments appeared to be hiding something beneath. She knew what nearly none of it meant, but she would learn.

The server leaned in to take Mireille's final plate, then Alder rose, inviting the court to a connecting chamber where music was to be played. When Mireille made to stand with the others, a dark, spiky shadow skittered out from beneath the table.

Before she had an instant to react, the thing launched itself toward her. Mireille rocked backward but the creature leapt at her chest, swinging a shadowy paw. Long claws caught the fabric of Mireille's gown as she dodged away. The creature was too fast, too unnatural. Mireille stumbled into her chair just as the dark-haired server's tray tumbled to the floor, sending shards of pottery flying. The woman had hold of the shadowy creature before another blink, and the thing shrieked out a horrible cry.

The cry fell silent just as the world went still. Even the echo of shattering glass abated. The shadow creature dropped from the motionless server's hands, but it did not run away. The creature did not move, only stared hungrily at Mireille. Beyond the glamour, it was wholly fae, a thing with too many limbs, a wrongness about it that could not be put to rights. It was a child's drawing of a nightmare, come to life. Mireille's gaze rose to find the prince at the opposite end of the table. He stood, as still as the world around them. Every fae present had risen to their feet—frozen as if time had stopped. A goblet rested on its side, the droplets of wine suspended mid-spill off the edge of the table. Mireille's fingers longed to reach for it, to test the drop. But all of it was real. So very, very real.

The prince stared back at her, his gaze for her alone. She managed not to breathe, which was useful, as it likely would have cut through the silence like a horrified gasp. Alder lifted a hand. The room's occupants remained frozen, but all else seemed to shift. The table, the dishes, every single object that separated the prince from Mireille, slid carelessly aside. A half dozen platters crashed to the ground as the table screeched to a halt, candelabra hit the floor and guttered out, and some of the fae in their fine gowns were splattered with cordial and fruit. The staff at the edge of the room made not a single move. Mireille wasn't certain they could.

The prince strode forward, lit only by the remaining torchlights on the wall.

In the moment, Mireille hadn't had time to realize the shadowy creature may have represented a political attack, that someone may have known she was to be his bride. But if the prince's act in response had been a warning, it was effective. Each fae became unfrozen as their prince moved past, even his sister, and each took a knee, their heads bowed low and eyes downcast, as solemn as death. His slow stride seemed to promise that whoever was responsible for the deed would pay.

Mireille's stomach swam, both from the shock and from the dizzying way the room had shifted. The prince stopped before her, and everything that was frozen resumed once more with the drip of wine echoing in Mireille's ears. Without a word, Alder held forward a hand. She took it. They would not be enjoying an evening of music, that much was clear. And though she wasn't certain she had a choice in the matter, she let him lead her from the room.

CHAPTER 3

Noal waited in the corridor outside the dining hall. When they strode past, he followed Mireille and the prince through the adjoining room and into a large, open space scattered with statuary.

The prince released Mireille's hand as he turned toward her and inclined his head. He seemed to be restraining a great deal of fury. "Noal will return you safely to your rooms."

"I'd prefer to walk with you. I was hoping for a tour," she said, mildly ill and shaky, and somewhat proud her voice did not reveal either. What she was truly hoping, was to not lose her chance to stay near him so that she might discover anything at all to help her kingdom out of a mess.

He frowned. "I have important tasks that must be completed—"

"Of course. The tour can wait. You may complete your tasks as needed and I'll simply watch while you..." She made a little fluttering gesture with her fingers to indicate his tasks, light and airy, as if they both weren't aware she'd just watched him destroy a dining hall.

He did not seem pleased by either the gesture or the

suggestion that she accompany him. "The information I intend to discuss with my staff is privileged. Though you are a guest here, even your own interkingdom policies would not permit an outside presence, regardless of our agreement. If you will allow Noal to return you to your rooms so that he and I may have a private word—"

"That is entirely understandable, and I assure you it's no trouble at all. I'll just wait over here by the sculpture until you're finished with the confidential bit with Noal." She brushed a hand casually over the fabric of her gown, where the lesser fae had left a tear. "I doubt anything will bother me while I wait. If it does, I'll be sure to scream."

His expression darkened.

She did not waver.

The prince flicked a gesture—considerably less carefree than her own—toward Noal, effectively ordering the man into a separate room. The door closed behind Noal and the prince as Mireille wandered nearer the statue, then she lifted her feet out of her slippers and rushed across the room. Ear pressed to the door, she held her breath to hear.

"...whoever did this and deliver them to me personally."

"Of course."

"She is under my protection. We are betrothed. I do not have to tell you the consequences should she be endangered again."

"Of course. I shall see to it straightaway."

"Noal."

"Highness?"

"You cannot possibly believe I will let you walk out that door without answering for the rest of it."

"I am unsure of what you're referring—"

"You know exactly what I'm referring to. But *by the wall*, I cannot understand what you were thinking."

"Of course. The princess's attire. It was entirely my

mistake. I was working under the impression such was the fashion in Westrende so I believed it fitting. It is our duty to make guests comfortable, after all, so of course only familiar fashions would do."

"You've been to Westrende," Alder snapped. "Recently. You know their fashion is no such thing. It was clear to me, as well as everyone in attendance, the intent of such a costume."

"I am unsure what—"

"Do not try me."

"Of course," Noal repeated. "Her highness's wardrobe will be remedied. Just as soon as the seamstresses are able."

There was a weighty pause. "*As soon as they are able?* So that is how it is, then? Betrayed in my own house by my own man."

Noal did not answer.

The prince's voice dropped low. "Do you think me so easily persuaded? That a bit of skin would tempt me to fall at her knees?"

A pause. "She is quite striking, is she not?"

There was the sound of something solid settling very heavily onto wood. When the prince spoke again, his resolve was evident. "That seals it. You have proven you cannot be trusted. No more traps for your prince—the prince, I'll remind you, to whom you've sworn allegiance. And from this night forward, no more gatherings. You will not parade her about or take risks with our treacherous court. In fact, dinner will be private, the lady and myself only. Should she attend a gathering, she will be on my arm through the entire event or she shall not attend at all."

Noal said, "I can see how that would be best."

The prince's tone dipped and Mireille had the sense he was leaning in to deliver his threat. "I will not forget whose side you are on."

"We are on the side of Rivenwilde, Highness. With respect."

He huffed. "*We* you say, as if the entire house were against me."

If Noal made a response it was silent. Then footsteps sounded and the prince's voice came nearer to the door. "I am Rivenwilde. You would all do well to remember it."

Mireille stumbled backward then ran as fast as she was able toward her spot by the far wall. When the door came open, she held her gaze on a tall piece of marble statuary in the shape of a woman, a bounty of fruit spilling over the carved arms and a fox curled around the figure's legs so that the tail hung over the base. She could feel the prince's eyes on her as he stood for a moment at the doorway. He closed the door with Noal inside, then strode toward Mireille.

Beneath the long skirt of her own gown, she shoved her feet back into her slippers. She kept her gaze on the statue, specifically the flowers and fruit, which somehow evoked the scent of early summer despite that they were merely cut stone. When Alder reached her side, Mireille said, "This is beautiful."

He did not reply.

"I've noticed a few recurring themes in the works throughout the palace." She glanced at him. "What is the significance of the orange blossom?"

It was the wrong question. His posture, already rigid, went more so, his wide shoulders drawn back and neck taut. "I must return to my tasks."

She straightened to face him, offering a small smile. "Of course. Do, go on. Pretend as if I am not even here."

He muttered, "*Of course,*" then turned to walk down the long corridor.

Mireille hurried to keep pace, concerned she might have pushed him too far by using the words Noal had repeated. But she had to push him enough to keep him at least a little off balance, or she would never find answers.

They traversed several rooms and corridors, passing dozens of closed doors before she said pleasantly, "While I eagerly await the coming tour—I suppose I would do well to be familiar with the expectations of your house in the meantime. Are there rooms that I am not to investigate? Areas that may be forbidden?"

"You are not imprisoned. You may go where you like."

"But not outside the walls of the palace," she said. "And not to court events."

He stopped so abruptly that she nearly stumbled into him. "You agreed to the bargain. Willingly."

"I have not changed my mind. I am only attempting to find my footing."

"There is nothing to find. Until the next moon, you are a guest here."

Afterward, Mireille would be taking on an entirely new role. There was a tiny line at the edge of his brow, as thin as one of his dark lashes. She fought the urge to reach out and touch it.

Something like ire sparked in his gaze. "Perhaps you should focus on ways to take your duties as guest more seriously."

He pointed toward what Mireille realized was a familiar corridor. "At the end of this passage, you will find the door to your suite."

Ignoring the dismissal, she glanced at the set of doors that had to be his. She said quietly, "It's very close to yours."

He went still.

"I suppose they are like our queen's apartments back home. Meant for your bride. So you might—" She made a little walking gesture with her fingers, indicating how a prince might make his way to his wife's room. "I wonder who might have stayed before me."

"Good evening, Your Highness."

"Mireille," she reminded him.

His jaw tensed. "Mireille."

"You said I may go wherever I like."

"You may. I suggest you learn to like your suite." He inclined his head shortly, then turned back the way they had come.

Mireille followed.

Hand on the lever of a door dark with age, the prince stopped to look down at her. Mireille was not a small woman but he managed to tower over her anyway. There was no possible way that he believed she'd misunderstood his dismissals. "This is my study."

"Oh," she said. "So, *anywhere*, but not"—she pointed toward the door—"*there*. Would you call the study forbidden, then?"

His gaze narrowed. She smiled sweetly.

After a moment, he unlatched the door, then held it open as he gestured her past.

She stopped in the center of the dimly lit space. It was exquisitely decorated in rich hues and dark finishes and smelled faintly of something warm and sweet. It was a very personal, intimate sort of space. She was surprised he'd let her in.

His low voice seemed to brush over her skin from where he waited behind her. "I'll remind you that you will not be able to repeat anything you've seen here. Investigations into my rooms will do you no good."

She did not turn to look at him. "I'll remind you that I am not a spy. I'm only interested in becoming acquainted with Rivenwilde." She did not say, *And you are Rivenwilde, after all,* because she had been, in fact, spying when she'd overhead the comment.

The prince walked past her toward his desk and she moved to peruse a wall of books. It was clear that he was endeavoring to stay within the bounds of courtesy and those of the laws of hospitality—he must, given that she was princess and equal to his station—but there was no question he found the entire situation trying.

What was less clear, was why he needed a princess that he did not seem to want.

"Is this your full collection? Or is there a library located elsewhere?"

Head down, hand spread over a document he appeared to read, he said, "I believe I was to pretend you were not here."

She could not help the smile that tugged at her lips. Reaching toward a book on the shelf, she glanced at him over her shoulder. "May I?"

He watched her face, not the finger hovering over a title. "You may take all the privileges due to a guest."

She dropped her hand. "I do not wish to take privileges. I would rather they were granted freely."

His eyes returned to the document. "Read any title you like. You will find no secrets on those shelves. I have nothing to hide that you might find there, nor on any shelf in this palace or its library."

She wandered close to his desk, her gaze tracing the lines of the fine script on the page. "No secrets, then. But I wonder if the tales are true." She leaned nearer to watch as the line of words grew beneath his pen. "Can you lie?"

The nib caught on the page for just an instant before resuming its path. "What is a lie but intent?"

She hummed. "And what is glamour if not a lie?"

The quill stilled. The prince looked up at her. "You have seen through our glamour from the start."

She reached forward, carefully brushing a finger over the edge of his brow where a small scar hid beneath that glamour, invisible to the eye but plain beneath her touch. "Then why does it remain between us?"

His reply was barely above a whisper. "That is not for you."

She drew her hand back, uncertain whether he meant the glamour or the touch. "How thoughtless of me. Of course not everything is meant for me."

In the candlelight, the darkness of his eyes seemed to shift —like pools beneath a night sky that begged to draw her in. She straightened away from him. He was right, the glamour had not been meant for her. It was only another tool of the fae, and if the prince wanted her to be drawn to him, he would not be trying so hard to push her away.

"Forgive me," she said quietly. "I will leave you to your work."

Halfway to the door, she stopped at the sound of his reply.

"Perhaps... a book might help to occupy your time. Feel free to take along whichever were of interest to you."

CHAPTER 4

Mireille had taken a pair of books from the prince's study that appeared well-worn. The first included diagrams of a variety of plants and their root systems, and the second was a thin volume of poetry in a language she was less familiar with. Perhaps it was true that she would not find his secrets, but it might at least bring her some understanding of the man. She could appreciate the responsibilities of a title and the desire to hold distance or withhold trust—the very behaviors she practiced with him—but Mireille could not help but wonder what else might be behind the prince's taciturn manner.

She wished very much that he had not brushed aside her comment regarding any princesses who might have come before her.

Back in her suite, Mireille sat with her feet curled up on the settee while Thomas settled in the chair nearby. Dressed in a dark blue coat and breeches, he appeared as dapper as any of the fae she'd dined with, though considerably more weary. She gave him a brief summary of her evening's events before asking about his own. "You seem to have survived, at least. Did all go well?"

He shrugged his shoulders, adjusting his jacket. "*Well* may be too strong a word, but I was able to gain my bearings a bit and met a few members of staff."

"Anything of use?"

"It seems the palace staff is eager to have you. So that's something. Past that, I'm not certain what either they or the prince gains from the bargain. Noal was keen to assist with anything I asked…"

"But?"

His gaze slid to hers. "I do not believe he's dressed you in the style of court."

Mireille nodded. "So it seems. I overheard the prince giving him a thorough set down. The household may be encouraging the prince in ways he is not comfortable with. Unfortunately, it's impossible to know if this makes them our allies or simply another obstacle to overcome."

He nodded, though his mouth had gone flat. "Evidently staff is also aware that the queen has shown interest in the relationship between Westrende and Rivenwilde. There is speculation as to how it might shape the future of the realm."

When Thomas went quiet, Mireille realized her hand had slid protectively over her throat. She dropped it. "What else?"

Thomas's finger tapped the plush arm of his chair. "It was brought to my attention that there is a lovely piano in the music room. Twice."

She frowned. "I've not played in years. How would they have guessed I once had an attachment to such a thing?"

"They've evidently made inquiries." He gestured to the console table near the door. "And look there."

Mireille followed his indication, finding the table had been set with a bowl heaped with oranges between a pair of orange blossom bouquets. "Well," she said. "We will certainly be looking into the history of oranges."

Thomas hummed in agreement, but it was not the satisfied sort. It was the sort that held an undercurrent of concern. If Mireille had to guess, she would say it was owing to the time they had left, and that it was already dwindling away.

But she did not have to guess. Thomas had told her repeatedly how displeased he was with her plan. He wanted her safe. He wanted her alive.

Fate save her, she was trying. The prince's reserve wasn't helping. He did not trust her, and she couldn't be certain it was merely due to her connection to his enemies in Westrende. That they had looked so deep into her past was worrying. Mireille hoped very much they had not looked as far into Thomas and his skillset, or his access to the palace and its staff might be cut off.

She said, "So, tomorrow night I attend a private dinner and you..."

"Find the dungeons," he finished.

She dropped her head back onto the settee. "Capital. All we need now is to figure out how to thwart a queen who is all-powerful."

"She's not all-powerful. Everyone has a weakness." Thomas stood. "Mine is cheese."

Mireille smiled up at the ceiling as Thomas made his way to the doorway. He sank easily to the floor in front of the door to the corridor, tucked a hand beneath his head, and crossed his legs at the ankles before his eyes slid closed.

It was midnight when Mireille rose from her bed. She had no need of a timepiece; it was always midnight when she rose. Bare feet gliding silently across the cool stone floor, she made her way to the door of her room. She did not step over Thomas, but stood very near his slumbering form. The understanding that he could not be awoken settled within her, and her body shifted. Drawn toward the corner of the room, she pressed her palm flat to the wall where no door should be. A hidden panel opened.

Mireille did not feel the surprise that should have come at her hand finding a panel her mind had not known was there.

She walked into the corridor. If anyone in the palace was present, Mireille was not aware. Her feet continued through the maze of corridors, taking her to an exterior palace wall. The palace was somehow more alive in the darkness, but she could not pause to consider why. She only continued through the corridors, past carvings that seemed to writhe, past gilded decorations and crawling vines. Her steps did not cease until a toe bumped against a tall arched window, open to the world beyond. Cool night air brushed over her skin, seeping through her thin shift. The sickly-sweet scent of hawthorn flowers on the breeze drew her forward. She leaned into the archway, only night air between her and the courtyard three stories below.

Mireille did not feel the fear that should have come.

In the distance, firelight dotted the horizon, the fae courtiers in their costumes and finery, dancing at a moonlit ball. She could hear their laughter, feel their revelry. Wind tugged at the hem of her shift and she swayed with the music, further toward the open air and the nothing below. She had no control.

The song of the fae whispered, beckoning her on. *Mireille*, it sang. *Mireille*.

Her bare foot lifted past the lip of the archway.

Mireille was unable to feel the dread that should have filled her, but she knew what was to come.

She stepped forward.

"Rei!" Strong hands gripped her shoulders, drawing her back just in time. Thomas, chest heaving, hands trembling, murmured, "I have you. There we go." He dragged her farther from the ledge, cursing and muttering about the sort of palace that would have open windows and an utter lack of guards.

Mireille did not feel the relief that seemed to swim through him, though she knew she would. He let go only long enough to wrap a dressing gown around her. "Come on, back to bed," he said, and he tugged the gown tighter before guiding her by the shoulders. "This was a close one. Tomorrow night, we're tying bells to your person."

IT WAS EARLY the next morning, wrapped in her dressing gown beneath several layers of blanket, that Mireille felt everything she should have the night before. It was never pleasant when the feelings returned, never left her unshaken to have lost all control. The hope that a bed inside the palace might be out of the queen's reach was gone.

She had woken to find Thomas's spot by the door empty. A large dresser had been slid across the room, covering the panel they'd missed in their initial inspection. A collection of delicate glassware was placed precariously near its edges, easily crashed to the floor should the dresser be jostled.

They should have found the panel. They had made a mistake.

They would have to do better.

Mireille called for tea, then searched the wardrobe for her most serviceable gown. She found a scrap of fabric to tuck into the low neckline of the bodice like a fichu, and in short order, she was prepared for the day.

Thomas met her near the library as planned, where they intended to scour the shelves for fae tradition, law, and history. Much of the outside world did not credit the existence of magic. To most, fae were only a tale of times past, a danger which had long ago been caged, which was how the fae queen had been so easily able to slip into the kingdoms she'd taken before Norcliffe. Few understood the laws that bound fae, and even less was known about how they spent their time. Mireille knew more than most, but it felt as if she knew nothing at all.

The library rose three stories, open in the center where arched beams draped with tangled ivies cut through the light from a ceiling composed of etched glass. A network of stairs and ladders wove between balconies and levels, and yet, many of the shelves remained bare. Likewise, despite the size of the palace, not a single other soul was present. Mireille's best chance to save her father and their kingdom should be there, within the massive fae library. But the scene was suspect.

Mireille glanced at Thomas, who was biting his lip. "Do you suppose..."

"Let's not suppose." He ran a palm over his neck. "We'll do well to remember we are no longer dealing with the expected. It would be foolish not to check here first."

"Right," she said. "Where shall we start?"

Lips pursed, he gestured vaguely toward the far wall. "You take that section, I'll try the second level."

They spent hours scouring the shelves for any hint of information helpful to their cause. Half the tomes were in languages Mireille had never seen, and what wasn't locked behind glass and marble was entirely useless for her purposes.

She was being pursued by the fae queen, a malevolent terror who wished to destroy Norcliffe and all that Mireille held dear, and nothing could be done to prevent the impending disaster. If Mireille did not find a way to subvert fae magic, to save her family and her kingdom, then nothing would be left. The queen would rise in power, gaining more authority with every crown she grasped and every castle she toppled.

Bargaining with the fae prince had been, quite literally, their last chance. And she could not even find a book on the cultural history of fruit trees. It was beginning to appear as if they'd never had a chance at all.

By the time tea was served, Mireille had nearly given up hope of finding information on fae law or tradition. "Perhaps he wasn't lying. Perhaps there's not a secret here among any of the shelves."

"So, where, then?" Thomas popped the last bite of a cucumber sandwich into his mouth. "The prince's suite?"

Mireille's own sandwich stuck in her throat.

He handed her a cup of tea. He said, "Well, *I* can't go in there."

"And you expect I can? That anyone would allow me to dance my way right over the threshold to his private chambers?"

The look he gave her said far more than any remark could have.

Mireille groaned. "Be reasonable, Thomas. It's not as if fae secrets will be bolted to the wall with a finely engraved plaque. *Here lies the knowledge of every fae conundrum known to man. Feel free to browse this register of twelve proven methods to trick a fae.*" The edge of Thomas's mouth twitched and, a bit overtired, Mireille plowed recklessly on. "Perhaps I'll find just the one I need now: A *detailed account for working your way into a fae prince's bedchamb—*"

Mireille squeaked and fumbled her teacup as a throat

cleared behind her. There was a flash of surprise in Thomas's expression before it smoothed to something more cordial, revealing that he had been just as unaware that they'd been approached. Mireille set her cup on the small table, then glanced at the fae now standing beside them.

The woman leaned forward as she replenished the tray. It was the dark-haired server who had saved Mireille from the shadow creature, and from the seatmate who had tried to trap her in a bargain, the night before.

"Forgive us," Mireille said. "I'm afraid... well, I'm afraid there's no excuse for it."

The woman offered a closed-lip smile as she worked.

Mireille tried again. "I want to thank you for last night. It can be quite difficult to navigate court life and it means a great deal that you were willing to come to my aid."

The woman only inclined her head. Mireille glanced at Thomas; he gave an infinitesimal shrug. Mireille reached forward, gently touching her fingertips to the woman's hand to still her work. When the woman met her gaze, her dark eyes seemingly free from pretense, Mireille asked, "What may I call you?"

The woman placed the tea pot on the table, then reached up to tap her fingers to her throat.

Mireille gestured with her reply. "In Norcliffe, we were taught a bit of signing. Is this version familiar to you?"

The woman responded with a gesture that appeared to mean, "well enough," then she glanced at Thomas, who held a book over his knee, and indicated for him to pass it over. When Thomas obliged, the woman pointed out the letters of a name.

"Kin," Mireille said.

The woman inclined her head again.

"Well, Kin, I am in your debt."

The sidelong glance she gave Mireille spoke volumes.

"Right," Mireille said. "I will remember not to offer my debts out so easily, as well as not agreeing to any sly bargains."

She gave a curt nod, then dipped her head as if to go.

"Kin." When she turned back, Mireille asked, "Would the law books be on the first level or the third?"

With the smallest upward tilt to the corner of her mouth, Kin indicated her burden of tea pot and tray as if to imply she could not answer.

"I wonder," Mireille said smoothly, "if the fae laws of hospitality would supersede any orders from your prince."

Kin's brow lifted playfully, then she turned to place the tray on a side table.

"Interesting," Thomas murmured.

Mireille grinned. "Indeed."

It was surely no accident that the fae secrets were tucked away. The morning search had been fruitless and frustrating and Mireille had no time to waste. They were going to have to use fae customs they did not entirely understand in order to gain any ground.

They followed Kin up a wide spiral staircase to a second story balcony where only a handful of bound volumes rested on a shelf. A pale stone ledge extended from the wall beneath the shelf, its supports carved into woody vines with wisteria draped over the edge. To one side rested a plush chair, beside it a small table.

Mireille bit her lip, exchanging a glance with Thomas, as they'd already checked the few books on the shelf. She said, "Anything on customs and traditions would be helpful as well, but what we would really like are the older texts. Thomas is a bit of a historian, you see, and this is his favorite pastime. I, on the other hand, could do with a primer on court etiquette and something detailing the royal code."

Kin nodded, tucking her dark hair behind an ear as she stepped closer to where Thomas stood by the ledge, his fingers tracing carved markings that Mireille could only assume were some sort of ancient script.

Shoulder to shoulder, Kin placed her hand over Thomas's. She guided his palm to lie flat against the stone. He started, his hazel eyes flicking to her face, then Mirelle sensed the tingling warmth of magic that rose from their connected hands.

Kin's fingers slid away, and beneath Thomas's palm rested bound linen pages, their script trimmed in red and gold. He went still for one very long moment before his own hand slid reverently down the page.

Kin placed her palm on the ledge beside the first book, and another rose to the surface. Her smile was soft as she crossed her wrists behind her back and strode toward the window, eyes on the distant trees.

Thomas was too still, too quiet. Mireille leaned nearer, glancing briefly at the tome Kin had apparently left for her. "Well?"

His laugh was small and breathless, attention never straying from the page. "I don't have any idea what it says."

Mireille could just make out the corner of Kin's mouth lifting where the woman stood facing the balcony. She had done what they had asked, fulfilled the wishes of the prince's guests. But she had not broken any trust; the fae secrets were just as far away as they had been.

Except that Thomas was no amateur historian. He excelled at breaking codes. Beside her, he said, "Another. Please. Same time period."

Kin turned, expression wary at the change in his tone, but Mireille only smiled and said, "See? He loves this stuff."

Late in the afternoon, after Thomas had exhausted Kin and devoured more texts than Mireille could count, Noal appeared to retrieve the pair. Mireille made a point to grouse about their lack of success.

"Was there something in particular you were searching for?" he asked.

Absently, she ran a thumb over a finely carved vine that edged the table. Every detail of the palace felt intentional, as if nothing had been left out. "Actually, several things. But I was wondering most of all about fae customs. The significance of certain flowers, for instance." The flowers were far less a concern than the stipulations of fae bargaining and the right of rule, but the blossoms seemed her most likely chance to gain Noal's trust, especially given the look he had shared with the prince their first night. When he did not respond, she tapped a fingernail against a small glass urn atop the table. "Can't find anything of the sort, despite all of these references."

Noal's expression remained level. "You wouldn't. They're in our hearts, practiced within our rituals. Our traditions are not bolted to the wall with a finely engraved plaque or listed on a register for all to see."

A small, choked sound came from the corner, where Thomas attempted to cover his laugh with a cough, likely at the man's reference to her earlier comment.

"Yes," Mireille said. "I can see how listing them out might be a problem. I wonder, then, how one might find the answer to those questions instead."

Noal did not respond.

"I suspect I will not find them with the prince."

Noal's attention seemed to sharpen on her. "Indeed, if one were to discover insight at all it would be with the heart of Rivenwilde. Your dinner with the prince approaches. Shall we return you to your rooms so that you may prepare?"

She leaned nearer, dropping her voice. "Truly? You've nothing to offer but obscure comments?"

"Not in the way of kingdom secrets, no."

Mireille narrowed her gaze. "Because you cannot reveal more or because you will not?"

"Precisely."

"I see," she said. "It appears we are left entirely up to our own devices."

BECAUSE OF THE ATTACK, Alder had changed the rules. Their dinner would be private. He was to meet Mireille at her suite, then walk with her to a secluded dining hall.

Dressed for the occasion in a gown that was far more elegant than the last—and with a much lower neckline, despite the prince's warning to Noal—Mireille stood in the center of her sitting room, watching as the door came open, well past when she was to expect the prince.

It was not the prince who entered, but Noal, dressed in his dark suit and perfectly tied cravat. "The prince has been detained with court business. Perhaps this evening's dinner would be better taken in your rooms. Shall I have it brought up straight away and send your regrets?"

She gave the man a patient smile. "I will wait for him."

Noal's expression did not waver. "It may be quite some time."

"I trust that the prince will keep his word. He will show eventually, and that is all that matters. I have nothing but time, after all." *And nowhere near enough of it.*

"Of course." Noal's hands unclasped to fall to his sides. "I will return when he is—"

"I will wait for him outside of—wherever he is."

That earned her a small twitch at the corner of his lips. "As you wish."

He led her to a gallery that looked out over the kingdom, a wide window before low stone steps that felt very quiet and still. "No one will bother you here. This is a private gallery reserved for His Highness."

Mireille drew her eyes from a view of expansive estates and lush forests. "You do not have to wait with me. I'm certain you've other matters to attend."

Noal inclined his head. "Should you need anything—"

Mireille waved his comment away. "I have it well in hand, though I do appreciate your concern. You'll recall, I am a princess as well. I'm used to waiting for selfish and stodgy royals with no regard for the schedules of others."

He appeared to swallow a sound but Mireille could not quite make out whether it was one of humor or shock. She suspected a man like Noal could not be easily shocked.

"Well, then, I will leave you to it." He gave a bow and walked from the room.

Hours later, Mireille still sat on a finely carved marble step watching as the sun began to set. Far in the distance, the treetops were tipped with a rosy gold. Her slippers were tucked neatly beneath her skirts, and well away from the ledge of the archway that opened into the coming night. Outside in the distance was a festival, its fae music drifting up to her on a jasmine-scented breeze. She would need to return to her rooms before midnight, but no matter how much the sound felt as if it were calling her, Mireille would not go. Not in the light of day when she had any choice in the matter.

Besides, if she stepped foot outside the castle, she would no longer be protected. The prince and his rules were all that was keeping her safe.

She was not certain how long he had been watching from the shadows, but when the sun had finally dipped below the trees, the last of its light a fading haze of color along the horizon, Mireille said, "It is quite a breathtaking view. I can see why you've chosen this as your sanctuary."

A moment of stillness followed in which she was not certain he would reply. Perhaps he had not meant for her to notice him. Perhaps, like her, he had felt the stillness of time, there at the dying of another day, too bittersweet to break. But he came forward, on slow and silent steps, to stand by her side.

Mireille glanced up at him. "Is it a festival to celebrate the change of seasons?"

His gaze remained on the fires in the distance. "A festival, yes. Marking the coming of winter... no."

She ran a hand over her bare arm. "I confess, it seems very strange to have stood in the Westrende forest where leaves seemed ready to fall and to experience that bite of wind, only to step through the wall to find, suddenly, surroundings like that of a hothouse. Will winter come for your lands soon?"

"One way or another, I suppose it will." His dark eyes met hers, and he held forward a hand.

Mireille took it, her bare palm sliding against his glove. They stood for a moment before the balcony. Perhaps Mireille imagined the sense of loneliness from him before he turned, placing her hand inside his arm to guide her to their promised dinner.

He led her to a room that was as spacious as the one in which they'd dined the night before, but instead of a long table lined with seating, there waited only two chairs at a table even longer. And the chairs at opposite ends, no less.

After Mireille was settled into her seat, Alder strode to the taller, more elaborate chair, clearly meant for a prince of the fae, its back a carved tangle of wood that mirrored his crown, its arms wrapping solidly around him before disappearing like roots into the floor.

Mireille examined the table setting as a server poured thick red liquid into her goblet.

"It is... very formal," she said to the prince, feeling the need to raise her voice to reach him at the other end. "This is surely not where you normally dine. Would you prefer to return to your usual dinners, with family and members of your court?"

"Most evenings, I do not dine with my... with anyone. This month, the celebrations, it is an unusual affair."

She cocked her head in interest, but he did not go on. Clearly, he was not going to make it easy to get close to him, even when she had him relatively alone. "Where, precisely, do you dine, then?"

"My study."

"Well, that sounds..."

He flicked a gesture at the wait staff.

"...cozy," Mireille finished.

The prince took a sip from his goblet.

"Can you tell me about your court? I would love to hear how your days are spent—"

The prince's goblet returned to the table. "I will not discuss matters of the court or my duties to the palace. You are not yet privy to kingdom affairs."

Mireille stared at him. He stared back. She said, "Noted. Are there any other topics that are forbidden?"

His expression hardened. She wondered if word had gotten back to him about their search in the library. She wondered if they'd gone too far on only their first day, revealed too much.

Alder waved the servers to proceed. The first two courses did not go any better. By the time they'd progressed to the third, both were speaking curtly, when they spoke at all, and it was clear the prince was itching to escape. He had likely expected her to give up waiting for him to meet her that evening at all. It may have been her fault that he felt pressed, but she could not be sorry for it.

"Dinner was," she started at the same time he said, "Perhaps we should retire—"

He broke off, something like frustration skittering over his expression before it disappeared.

"Yes," Mireille said. "We should absolutely excuse ourselves early." He began to stand and she added, "Best we leave plenty of time for the tour."

He froze midway to his feet, bent awkwardly over the table as he glanced up at her.

He was likely going to hate her before the month was up, but Mireille only smiled. "You have the time, do you not, given that you had planned to spend it here, with me? Per our agreement."

A muscle near his jaw ticked. He straightened to standing.

Mireille waited, his name hovering on the tip of her tongue. She would use it, as often as she must.

"Yes," he finally answered. "The tour."

His tone implied something along the lines of *let us get this over with* but it was not the time to quibble. She'd won a victory, minuscule though it was.

CHAPTER 5

It did not take long to realize the prince intended to give Mireille an abrupt tour. He shared little to no detail or history for each of the many rooms as they walked through the palace. "The blue room," he said. "The conservatory." Past a circular chamber, he gestured vaguely. "The east wing." Then, "Staff quarters."

But when they came to a music room, Mireille stopped, peering through the doorway into a lavish space adorned with rich blue draperies, gold-trimmed furnishings, and filled with instruments that appeared to be of the finest craftsmanship she'd ever seen. Her gaze snagged on the sleek grand piano inlaid with a vining pattern of leaves and blooms, and her heart twisted.

It felt like only a moment, but the prince must have noticed. "Would you like to play?"

"No." Mireille's words were too faint. She forced herself to look away from the instrument—and at him. He had extended an olive branch in the one area she did not wish to venture. She couldn't know if the house staff had told him of her history, or if he'd only seen her response to the instrument. She said, "I haven't played in years," as she tucked her hand into the crook of his elbow. "Come, there must be much more to see."

His dark eyes slid from her face, then he turned, making no comment on her evasion. They passed through several more rooms before a large portrait gallery caught Mireille's attention. "May we?" she asked with a glance toward the prince. He inclined his head, but only drew his arm from hers, freeing her to move as she wished while he waited in the corridor.

Mireille wandered slowly through the room, taking in compositions that revealed very little of fae life. Nowhere in sight was a battle scene, an interior of everyday life, nor even an arrangement of flowers. The works, it seemed, were merely a record of faces, various figures standing in the center of cold spaces, in decidedly austere jackets and trousers or serviceable gowns, a pedestal or seat in a few, the occasional vague archway behind, as if in concession. It did not dampen Mireille's interest in the least.

She strode forward, mesmerized by the unparalleled skill of the artist. The strokes were loose and feathered, and yet hit so perfectly as if to disappear. Her eyes could not stay landed on any particular detail, for every other detail was too fine not to follow to. "Remarkable," she whispered, finding herself drawn closer and closer as she went. The corner of the mouth, the tilt of an eye; they seemed to contain the very soul of the subjects, distilled to their essence.

Her steps froze. She turned to face what may have been the most impressive portrait of all.

In his spot near the entrance, the prince had gone suddenly too still. But Mireille could not be made to look away from the wall.

The figure in the painting stared down at her, as large as life. He stood tall and slender, long, fine hands with elegant fingers that spoke of grace and beauty, and richly dressed despite the wardrobe being carefully nondescript. Dark hair beneath a crown of bone-line tangled spikes framed a face whose expression was that of a man certain he's been done wrong. His posture seemed to judge the viewer, even as his gaze seemed to smolder with intent. He was handsome, as handsome as any man Mireille had ever seen. And yet, the portrait spoke of a terrifying power. It held a dark and deadly weight. A secret.

The portrait was of the prince with whom she'd just sparred over dinner, so well painted that as Mireille studied it, the corner of his lips seemed to tip into the hint of a smile.

She blinked, resisting the urge to step back. But the painting appeared as it had before, unsmiling, foreboding. There was no wicked smile curving at the edge of his lips at all. It was only a portrait, no more than pigment and oil.

At the entrance, its subject waited in the flesh. He had spoken not a word, but watched her with a very particular sort of stillness.

Mireille smoothed a palm over her skirt, thoroughly burying her unease before rejoining him. He was to be her husband if she had any hope of stopping the queen. She would not fear his power when he had not attempted to use it against her.

"Such an interesting collection," she said.

"Does it please you?"

She gave him a shallow smile. "The palace is stunning, all of it. The flowering vines and statuary, grand halls, intimate drawing rooms, and here, a gallery filled with exquisitely skilled work... I would be very hard to please indeed if I could not be happy with a place such as this."

His gaze stayed on her as they walked. "That was an evasion."

She pressed her lips. They passed an open balcony,

revealing a starless sky that had darkened to a blue so deep it was nearly black. "It is very beautiful. Leaving behind a family and a kingdom is no easy thing. I suppose it would be easier if one were to be assured those were safe. But I cannot fault your palace, Alder." At her use of his name, a shiver seemed to run through him. Mireille found she did not hate that at all. But it was not the time to put away difficult discussions. "From my perch inside the marble cage, your land seems lovely as well."

His voice was low. "I did not trap you in a cage. You were free. You stepped into it of your own accord."

She hummed her agreement. "And my only way out, it seems, is to marry you."

The prince did not respond. Decidedly so.

"You needed a princess. Had I not come, you would have taken any other with the same title. To overcome your battle with Westrende and destroy the barrier that is the wall? To unrend the kingdoms, unbind your power, and crush them beneath the terrible weight of fae magic. Is that why I am here?"

"You are here because you chose it." Then, as if he could not quite seem to help himself, he snapped, "You think me incapable of any act but destruction? That I am as corrupt as the tales say?"

One of her brows lifted. "Would you want me to admit such a thing?"

"When I ask a question of you, I would want that you could say yes or no without fear."

"You do not trust me. You shut me out the moment I inquire about the slightest detail. You want something, need something from me owning to my station, but you do not want to marry me."

His jaw flexed.

"I did come willingly, as you say. And yet, you accepted the bargain. A bargain in which I have only the choice to become your bride or to break our agreement and end up your prize." His eye twitched. "There," she said. "I see you, Alder. I understand that you do not want me. Not as your prisoner and not as your wife. You will not tell me why. So how do I win in such a situation? How, before the next moon, do I choose correctly?"

He straightened, the action drawing him away from her in a way that made her aware just how near they'd become. "There is no winning. You have already chosen. When moontide comes, the wedding ceremony will take place."

So, he thought making the bargain was where she'd gone wrong. Perhaps it was true. But Alder did not know that outside the protection of his palace waited a fate far worse than any she might face with him.

THEY WERE quiet as they walked back to the wing that held their suites. Unwilling to reveal their hands, unable to back down, they were resigned to their situation, and possibly a little sheepish about the weaknesses they'd just revealed. At least, Mireille knew she was.

It was time for a change in tactic if she had any hope of breaking through his façade.

There were no footmen, no courtiers, no other present in the corridors aside from Mireille and the prince. She wasn't certain if the others were in another part of the castle, or out for the festival, but the halls felt strangely quiet and still. If she had her bearings correct, the walls they strode between laid directly below the corridor outside the prince's rooms. She glanced at the prince.

"Ask." His tone was polite, and after a few strides without a reply, he gave her his gaze.

Her cheeks did not flush to be caught staring so openly, but it was a near thing. She held his gaze. "I was wondering whether these rooms lay beneath my suite."

"They do," he said.

"Then, likewise, yours, since they are connect—"

"One final stop?"

She blinked. Bringing up their connecting chambers more than once may have come across as an all-too-eager interest in his suite, or perhaps his staff had shared what they'd overheard in the library. But Mireille suspected she was being shut down anytime she strayed near the subject of the women whose betrothals had surely come before her own.

The prince only drew them toward a pair of tall, elaborately-carved doors. There was a moment of hesitation before he stepped away from her to push wide the door. It opened into a massive ballroom. The sight took her breath. Outside, the moon had risen. Pale marble limned by moonlight from a row of arched doorways on the far wall covered the entire space. The opposite walls were lined with tall mirrors, creating a silvery glow that shifted with Mireille's every step.

Faint music rose over the balcony like a whisper carried on the cool night air. She walked forward, her reflection keeping pace on every side, and she was helpless to prevent the grin that parted her lips. She spun, a bit giddy with the delight of it. The moment was so perfect, so lovely, that it did not seem real. Of all the beauty she'd experienced in his palace so far, this was the finest, made ethereal by the light and the music and the mirrors in the night air.

She remembered she was not alone, and paused her swaying to ask, "It is breathtaking, is it not?"

The prince's dark eyes stayed on hers, and though he did not answer, he moved slowly toward her.

"Come, won't you dance with me, here in the moonlight while the palace sleeps?" she dared to ask.

"The palace is not asleep."

Her smile widened. "Pretend. Imagine with me that we are not a prince and princess, that there is no bargain and that we have never been at odds."

He frowned. It did not make him any less handsome.

Mireille held her hand forward, and he took it, if reluctantly. She drew him nearer, her voice dropping. "Do you never relish a private moment? With every day surrounded by courtiers, by structure and formality, rarely alone to just..."

"Dance in the moonlight?" His voice was even, but not cold. He did not seem to find the moment unpleasant, and a bit of his surliness faded away as they stood, fingers entwined.

"No," she said softly. "I suppose you do not." She bit her lip. "But tonight, with me, you will."

Mireille guided his hand to her waist, taking position. For a heartbeat, she only stared up at him, unsure whether he would play along. But the music rose far in the distance, and he took the first step in rhythm with the soft, sweet fae melody.

He was a fine dancer. Graceful and fluid, seemingly aware of her in a way that made her own steps easy. His grip was steady against her waist, his other hand a practiced lead. They spun through the ballroom, gliding over the polished floor like seabirds skimming smooth waters.

She had not danced in ages, her kingdom under threat and her people in fear. She had not stood close to a man who was not her guard, or her friend, or her father. Alder was very a much a man, despite that he was fae. Tall, strong, and competent, and not quite so prickly once he'd relaxed into the motions. His gaze fixed on her, and the ballroom seemed to fade away. The song came to an end but Mireille did not want to let go. She did not want to return to the way things were, to thinking about what was to come, the worry about her people and her family. When he began to pull away, she held fast, not stepping backward, her hand remaining clasped in his. She needed him. She needed this.

Their eyes locked. "Stay with me," she whispered, though certainly she must have meant to add *for one more dance*.

Something shifted in his gaze. Magic perhaps, some hint of glamour or power, flickering beneath the influence of fae music and moonlight. His expression did not change, but his attention was on her so thoroughly that the atmosphere did.

In the distance, a new song swelled, carried to them on sweetly scented air. Alder's gaze remained on Mireille as his hand slid up to her shoulder blade, in preparation, she thought, for the new dance position. The cut of her dress was low, and a shiver ran through her as his gloved fingers grazed her bare skin. His lips parted, as if to speak her name, and Mireille felt herself tipping her head toward him. They were so close that the breath he released brushed over her skin.

"Your Highness."

The voice from the doorway broke whatever spell had come over them, and Alder went suddenly stiff. He dropped his hands. "What is it?"

The uniformed fae bowed deeply, in a move that spoke of regret. "Apologies, Your Highness, but there is in issue that requires your attention."

"I'll be right there." He seemed to shake himself before taking a step back from Mireille. Tone gone tetchy, he said, "I shall return you to your rooms, Your Highness."

At first Mireille chalked his tone up to the shock of interruption. But his conversation was noticeably curt as they made their way to her suite, and the rigid posture and obvious distance he held between them felt more like a rebuke. Mireille had been so close to... *something*.

Her time was running out. She needed to uncover the

prince's secrets, and the secrets of his people, to find a way to save her own. She needed him to need *her*. And not merely because she was a princess.

But Alder was protecting himself and his secrets. It was clear he hadn't meant to slip. He must have realized he had nearly let her in, and he likely had no intention of dropping his guard again.

It was clear that Mireille had just lost any footing she'd gained.

<h1 style="text-align:center">CHAPTER 6</h1>

At midnight, Mireille rose from the wide, plush bed once more. Her booted foot slipped between the scattering of metal and glass trinkets Thomas had spread over the floor without a whisper of noise. With nothing in her wardrobe but flimsy night dresses and elaborate gowns, she had taken a pair of his trousers, rolled at the waist, and a knotted-up shirt. Still, they had been certain there was no means for her escape.

She stood in the darkness of the still room. She could feel the soft weave of the rug beneath her toes, could hear the slow steady breath of Thomas in his spot by the door.

Thomas was thorough. After the panel had been discovered, there were no other exits he hadn't blocked. None aside from the passage meant for a queen—the door between Mireille's suite and the prince's that had been sealed by powerful fae magic. Magic a human princess could not break.

She moved soundlessly toward the door anyway. It was tall, half again her size, and carved with intricate vines and leaves. She placed a palm to the wood. Her pulse beat against its grain. For one beat of her heart, Mireille's awareness of the room disappeared, then she was back, trapped in the state of semi-consciousness she'd been in before. The leaves seemed to have shifted beneath her palm, and the door fell open into a short, dark passage. Mireille's feet drew her forward.

Mireille had not felt the fear that should have come when she'd nearly stepped into the night air off a balcony, and she did not feel the fear of stepping over the threshold into the room of the most powerful fae in Rivenwilde. She should have, she knew that, but it changed not a thing.

The room was finished in dark wood and trimmed in shades of green. Tapestries lined the walls, embroidered with deep green and gold, blue-green draperies hung loose over finely carved windows open to the night sky, and a pair of settees were scattered with velvet pillows. A single bed centered the far wall, empty of occupants. A plush chair rested in the corner, a bright strip of silk draped over the arm. Near the door through which Mireille had entered, halfway between her and a wide fireplace, sat a writing desk. Atop its surface, the flickering light of a single taper glinted off a glass inkwell and the silver blade of a paper knife. The taper was the only light aside from the blue-silver glow of the moon.

The prince sat in a chair near the empty hearth. Dressed in trousers and a loose shirt, the sleeves rolled up his forearms where he held a leather-bound book, he glanced up distractedly.

His gaze went dark.

Mireille could not decipher whether it was owing to the sight of the woman who was to be his wife in such a manner of apparel greeting him like a wight in the small hours or something more along the lines of a suspected assassination attempt, but the prince seemed to take either outcome as an a threat. He stood, the book he'd held sliding quietly onto the padded chair. He spoke not a word, but the warning in his gaze said volumes.

He was the prince of Rivenwilde. His power was so great that it could crumble the palace beneath Mireille's feet.

Against every scrap of her will, all while knowing it would be her end, she felt herself press forward. In a few short steps, near the edge of the desk, her hand reached past the inkwell.

Her fingers curled around the handle of the paper knife.

The grip was slim, cool against her flesh.

The prince's dark gaze tracked the movement, his own fingers curling tighter in tandem with hers. He held no weapon in his fist. Only magic. Fathomless power.

Mireille would lose.

But Mireille was not willingly playing the game. Her movements were decided by the fae queen. The queen's magic had drawn her from bed, had opened the sealed door, and had brought her to stand before a prince. It would see Mireille done in just as efficiently.

Before Alder made a single step forward, as he watched and waited as if to see how she might attack, her fisted hand raised. The knife did not aim for the prince, as he might have expected. The knife stabbed toward Mireille's own chest.

There was an instant in which time seemed to slow, the flash of realization coming to Alder's dark eyes that it was not, in fact, an attempt on his life. Then he lunged.

In the space of a heartbeat, Mireille was flat on the floor. The blade was knocked from her hand, clattering to the plank before it had hit its mark. The prince of Rivenwilde splayed over her, his magic and his body a heavy weight pinning her down, pinning down the magic running through her. It was as if she were buried beneath the earth itself, as if she could not find her body or her will. Neither Mireille nor the prince had spoken a word.

One side of her face was pressed to the floor. His cheek brushed the other. Against her ear, he whispered her name.

A shiver ran through her, deep and rich, and not at all reassuring, as it was suffuse with fae power.

Mireille snapped back to herself with a gasp, the queen's hold upon her broken. Her hands began to tremble, her heart to race. She had nearly met her end, at the invisible will of the fae queen, or at the very real, very tangible hands of a fae prince. It had been that close. And with it, the end for all of Norcliffe.

Overtop her, the prince exhaled roughly. Mireille managed to make a sound, not a particularly dignified one, and his grip on her slid from irons into something more like an embrace.

But his hold was not precisely what one might call gentle. "*Can you lie*, you ask me," he said, low against her ear. "*Can you lie?*" His fingers tightened for one instant against her bare arm then disappeared from her skin entirely. "As you masquerade before me, nothing but lies and deceit tied to a wire crown."

She barely had time for confusion to settle in before he was standing over her, staring down like she had betrayed both the man himself and his kingdom.

"This entire time, the bargain, the storytelling, all of it a ruse to get beneath my roof. And for what? To buy favor from the queen? Did you think I would not know? The seal on that door was formed by my own magic. Not a single fae might break through, except one as powerful as I, a royal. Did you think I would never guess? That by merely walking through that boundary you would not reveal your ties to *her*?"

Her, Mireille's mind repeated. *A royal.* He thought her in league with the queen. It was no wonder had offered her no trust.

Mireille rolled smoothly onto her feet, the way she'd been taught as a girl, ready to defend herself, to fight her way out of whatever sort of tussle she was about to be in. Because if her frantic heart and panicked limbs wanted anything, it was to act, to release the fear and emotion that had been trapped within. It did not matter that it was not the prince who had caused her situation. "A ruse?" she said. "You think this was a jape? A little lark for a bored princess with nothing else to do?"

"Clearly I do not think it a jest. I think it an act of treason."

Her hands balled into fists as her voice raised, any hint at discretion having deserted. "Treason? This has naught to do with you, or your kingdom. My only desire has been to save myself and my own people."

He leaned forward, voice a dagger. "Her magic is all over you."

Mireille's mouth came open to explain, to reveal what a monster the queen truly was, but before a word could escape, Thomas burst into the room.

Hair disheveled and collar askew, one arm braced against the door frame, the other positioned in a way that may have appeared it was securing his breeches, Thomas stood, his wide eyes darting from Mireille to the prince, then the blade on the floor.

The prince shot a look at Mireille that held something of shock and, possibly, accusation. It was then, she thought, that he realized what she was wearing.

Mireille flicked a meaningful glance at Thomas but he apparently had no intention of quitting the room. "He guards my door," she said defensively. "To prevent... nighttime wandering."

"Well, it was certainly well done of you," the prince snapped.

Thomas straightened.

"Don't—" Mireille started but before she was able to speak further, to describe the magic that came over anyone while the spellbound Mireille was in the room and how

Thomas had done all he could in such a situation, the prince was well into another tirade.

"Coming here to trespass and what—rummage through our libraries? Is that what you looked for? An answer to some riddle of hers? And what choice do I have in the matter? I must, against my wishes, entertain these bargains—these utterly foolish offers—endlessly. All because of single curse. Because of one fool act in one fool court." He carried on, his fury a rumble of power through the room. "I knew not to trust it. So eager to wed a prince. And now here you stand, your ties to her as clear as that fetching smile and captivating gaze my court goes on and on about. As if I cannot see with my own eyes. As if I need reminding." Mireille resisted the impulse to feel even remotely flattered. The prince shook his head once, swift and sharp. "All of you, Westrende and beyond, inventing your stories to scare children, warnings of how the fae are so scheming and devious, nothing but trickery. When it is you, in every single instance, every opportunity made or stolen, doing wrong by *us*." His gaze snapped to hers, angry and expectant.

She crossed her arms, realized it was not the thing to do in a thin shirt, then dropped them again. "I bargained with you as fairly as any fae. I have not once told a lie." At his incredulous look, she amended, "To you." And then, "About this."

He scoffed.

Her voice dipped. "Had I any other choice, trust that I would have taken it." When he showed no sign of relenting, no interest her explanations, she could not help but add a sharp, "You speak to me of your innocence while you hold Westrende prisoners under your very roof."

He moved toward her like the snap of a sail in storm winds. "You speak to me of captives as you gave yourself to us willingly."

"You."

His face pinched. "What?"

"I gave myself to *you*."

He drew back, a fraction of the heat seeming to drain from his posture. His throat moved in a swallow, but his tone did not entirely gentle. "Why was I not told of your connection to her?"

"It is not what you think. I have no bargain with the queen. I am here only to save my people. She wants Norcliffe." And she wanted Mireille.

His expression darkened. "You expect me to trust you. Knowing you walked through that door and—and—" He glanced at the paper knife in evident disgust. "You brought her into my palace."

Mireille ran a hand over her arm, then glanced at Thomas, who stood in silent support. "It was my hope that she could not reach me here. And I never suspected a door secured by magic could be opened by my own hands, so I certainly did not expect that she... that we would end up in your suite. She's never... I didn't realize her power ran so deep. I believed it was only the other entrances we needed to worry about, ones not sealed by magic. We covered the hidden panel as soon as we discovered it the night before."

The prince's reply swift, his words for Mireille but a good deal of his anger aimed unfairly at Thomas. "This has happened before?" When she didn't answer, he leaned in, voice low. "You are under my protection."

It was not simply her trespass, but his vow that had him so angry, then. If his guest was not kept safe, he would be breaking an ancient fae tenant. Mireille did not think that could be helped, but if she was able, she would give him an out. "This is my burden. It has nothing to do with you and I will not ask another to bear it."

He straightened, his manner never so princely as in that

moment. "If the burden was truly yours alone, then your man need not sleep at your feet like a dog."

Mireille flinched.

Thomas moved forward, clearly prepared to defend his position, but Alder raised a hand in warning. The prince said, "This discussion is over. I will oversee these... nighttime wanderings myself." His fingers flicked a dismissal and, without another word, he turned his back on the pair.

CHAPTER 7

The prince's words had felt like a slap. It hadn't mattered that Thomas had vowed to protect her of his own free will, that protecting her was a step toward protecting their kingdom. It was that Thomas and every other person who cared for Mireille and for Norcliffe were made to suffer because of what the fae queen was trying to do. It was that nothing could be done to stop it.

Alder did not owe Mireille kindness or understanding. She knew that. She'd entered his bedchamber, kept her secret from him and, though she hadn't realized it possible, had put him at risk from the queen's magic. But she could not let go of the fact that Alder, too, was fae. Fae, like the queen who had destroyed everything, mercilessly tearing the future from everyone Mireille loved.

He could not be trusted. No fae could. And yet, she felt ill at her own part in all of it. She tossed and turned, sending Thomas back to his own rooms, and by the time morning came, Mireille was a wretched mess. She had to make it work, had to find a way past their distrust, to melt his defenses. And she had a mere month to do it.

She'd managed only to don a gown and get her hair in decent order when there was a sharp knock at her chamber door. It was not the knock she'd grown accustomed to from Noal, so she crossed to the entrance to open it instead of calling out. When she did, the prince stared back at her.

He did not appear to have weathered the night as poorly. He was just as handsome and put together as always.

Mireille inclined her head. "Your Highness."

His jaw ticked, presumably at her formality. He bowed, then held forward his arm.

Mireille only looked at the proffered limb.

He cleared his throat. "I am willing to answer at least one of the many concerns you have brought to my attention. If it pleases you."

His tone made clear he meant something more along the lines of *that you have badgered me with incessantly since you arrived, and in fact, on several occasions, used to doubt my character* instead of *brought to my attention*. Or some such intimation, Mireille wasn't certain.

She straightened. "It does please me." In fact, she would have liked answers to all her concerns, but more than that, she needed any time he would give her. Grabbing a shawl Thomas had managed to obtain from a member of the staff, Mireille tucked her hand into the crook of the prince's arm and closed the door behind them.

At the end of the corridor, he led her down a wide flight of stairs that opened into a massive chamber, then through several more corridors cooled by the shade of endless creeping vines. The walk carried on for so long that she was sure it must be as far as possible from the entrance to the palace. When they finally slowed at a large archway that opened into an atrium, Mireille had the unsettling sensation of realizing her assumptions were in fact very, very wrong.

She stared across the space at a figure that appeared to be

dressed in the uniform jacket of Westrende red and gold. The man's legs were stretched out before him, boots polished to a shine. There was a thick book in his hand, and a glass of amber liquid resting on the small table beside him.

Mireille's gaze shot to the prince.

"Go on," he said. "Speak with him."

The words were plain enough. Mireille was meant to satisfy her concerns so that she might never accuse him again. She swallowed down her reply, stepping forward into the open room.

As she approached, she took in the scene. Sunlight streaming through a tall window was cut by palm leaves, throwing long lines of shadow across the man and the plush golden chair. His hair was golden as well, bright and clean, the trim of his silk suit straight and fine, his flesh appearing not only undamaged but full with health. All of this came as a surprise, not because she'd come across the man in a fine fae palace, but because the man in question was *human*. A prisoner.

He was a Westrende official. Mireille had met the man at a long ago function. She stopped before his chair, her breath caught in her chest, and he glanced up distractedly from his book.

"Lord Cadby."

"Princess," he said with a shocked smile. "What a joy it is to see you!" He began to stand, but his expression fell. He glanced anxiously through the room. "No," he said, "it would not be a joy, would it? Has Norcliffe been taken? Are your people well?"

Mireille knelt at his feet. "Cadby, how long have you been here?"

His bright brown eyes returned to her. "Two years now? I'm afraid it's hard to say. Things were a bit fuzzy for a while. Got into trouble, made some bad trades."

"A fae bargain? That's why you're here?"

Lord Cadby frowned. "It is, Highness. And there are more of us, still. Lords and ladies of Westrende, officers of the court, anyone of noble blood or with ties to a would-be king. I pray that is not how it happened for you."

"Something of the sort." She glanced toward the archway, but Alder's face was too shadowed to clearly make out. "I have an arrangement with the prince. I must become his bride by the turn of the moon, or break our agreement and join you and the others as a prisoner."

Lord Cadby breathed out a curse and leaned forward to take her hand. "Oh, Highness."

"Norcliffe has been under siege from a greater foe than him. And I'm afraid, my lord, that should our venture fail, it will not be my life alone at risk."

He whispered, "What can I do?"

"I need whatever information you can provide of the workings of fae bargains, any weakness of the prince, how we can use the magic that holds together the Rive in a way that might help protect our own kingdom. We are desperate for any scrap of knowledge that might break the fae's hold on Norcliffe."

He squeezed her hand. "I fear it is not so simple. The prince is tied by the Rive, and his kingdom is tied to him. The fae are divided as much as any kingdom. His court trapped, and the queen's court working to keep them that way." He shot a glance through the room, then leaned closer. "If the Rive comes down, the court of Rivenwilde will be in danger. It protects them as much as it keeps them caged."

"But that is what he wants. The prince has claimed to desire nothing more than to be set free."

"No," he said. In the archway, Alder stepped from the shadows, and Lord Cadby released Mireille's hand. "I don't trust him, Highness, I don't. But there is more going on than we've been told. Something else binds him as well."

Mireille had the same feeling, because despite their betrothal, the prince did not seem to want her too near. Mireille recalled his words from the night before, how one fool act in one fool court evidently led to him having to entertain offers of marriage. She wondered how many princesses were being held within the palace. She wondered whether they sat in sunshine reading books, or if they had met a fate far worse.

She stood. "Thomas is with me. I will send him to you. We will see what might be done to return you home."

Lord Cadby shook his head. "It's too late for that. And, though I don't deserve your kindness, I hope that you'll grant me leave to offer my support."

Mireille drew a steadying breath. "I would count myself lucky to have it."

MIREILLE HAD, perhaps, discovered the prince was not as ruthless as he seemed, but she did not say so on their return. He was still holding citizens of Westrende captive, bargain or no. He was still fae.

She still had to marry him.

He left to attend court business and Mireille, alone while Thomas did his best to investigate the goings on with the palace staff, wandered through the palace.

She traversed the corridors and climbed the grand stair, feeling turned around and out of sorts by the palace's layout. It was as if the rooms shifted about her, and she could never quite place where she was meant to be. When she turned the corner into a wide hall scattered with columns, Mireille's steps faltered.

Across the hall rose a pair of massive doors, seemingly carved out of the same strange stone that made up the filigree wall. Unlike the boundary wall, the doors revealed no glamour, only a pale polished surface carved into scenes from what Mireille could only imagine was very long ago. Their beauty drew her nearer, but with an undeniable sense of unease. There was something terrible about the carved figures; while a marvel of craftsmanship, their subjects were too real, their torment and anger palpable.

A rearing horse rose tall, its foreleg reaching off the surface and its eyes rolled wide. The man on its back was barely visible, but he, at least appeared human, face a rictus, longsword in hand. Fae warriors surrounded him, their magic seeming to tingle over Mireille's skin. She did not want to touch the doors, exactly, but she could not seem to prevent her hand from lifting, her palm expecting cool stone but finding only warmth.

The door eased open beneath her touch. Mireille swallowed and drew her hand free. Her tingling fingers curled into her palms, and her heart beat a warning in her ears. Still, her feet moved forward, into the darkness waiting on the other side.

A shaft of light cut through the space, leading her onward. The echo of her footfalls sounded far away, and the focus of the room was farther than any palace ballroom or hall Mireille had yet seen.

She did not cross it. Because over the dark stone floor was a fracture that rent the room. Stones rose beside it, jagged and uneven, their edges sharp. Blackness was all that could be seen in the space between, like a chasm despite that, surely, there would be rooms below. On the other side of the room, at the end of the split, was the Riven Court throne. It, too, was jagged and broken, its majestic spires incongruent and off-kilter, the light and shadows only making the scene worse.

A prickle ran down her spine. Very little was known of the magic that had split the kingdom of Westrende from that of the fae. Mireille was a royal, and as such usually afforded more details, but even she had been able to uncover aught else. It was said that the thrones of Westrende and Rivenwilde were tied, and while rumor vowed ill-luck was all that had prevented a new king from rising to power in Westrende, Mireille's friends seemed to think it was something more.

In Westrende, investigations into the illnesses and accidents that had stalled eligible bloodlines from coming into power had led only to dead ends. Lord Cadby had told her other royals were being held, anyone with bloodlines related to the king, and Thomas had reported hints from the fae that the prince was bound by more than simply bargains.

Alder had said he was trapped. Westrende was quietly losing kingdom officials.

Mireille ran a sweat-slicked palm over her skirt. She had witnessed very much the same sort of events in her own kingdom, at the hands of a fae queen. Perhaps she had misjudged much more than she knew.

A far-off bang echoed through the room, recalling Mireille of the dangers of exploring a fae palace. She backed toward the door, then let herself out, willing her pulse to steady.

Hours later, Mireille sat alone before a wide balcony with a luncheon of pastries worrying her lip. It was unlikely that Lord Cadby's warning and the information Thomas had discovered were unrelated. But she would have to uncover the missing connections herself. She had decided to attempt the library once more when a slender mink leapt onto the balcony railing. Mireille let out a small, startled sound, certain the creature had not been there before..

It was a great distance to the ground below the balcony.

Perhaps it had had been hiding near one of the water features. The mink stared back at her. Mireille sighed. "Never mind me. I feel as if I'm losing my senses, the way the décor seems to shift and creatures appear from nowhere around here."

The mink gave Mireille the sort of a look that might have been an eye roll from another creature. It raised onto its hindquarters and licked its paw as if it had no further interest in her, but when Mireille made to stand, the air shimmered around the creature. In the next blink, the mink was gone. In its spot stood the prince's sister.

Mireille sat heavily back into her seat. She lifted a hand, but it sort of hovered there, unsure what action might make the event she just witnessed disappear from existence as Nisha watched her. Mireille wasn't certain she'd understood such a transformation was possible, even if she knew the immense power of the fae.

The prince's sister crossed the space, the diaphanous hem of her ivory gown swirling in her wake, then, giving the tray of almond pastries an unimpressed glance, took the seat opposite Mireille. Though she had been a fur-covered only moments before, her fae hair was perfectly coifed, held back from her face by a series of small braids laced with silver wire and tiny gems. There were no twigs or leaves clinging to her as had in their last meeting, nor any sign of the outrage she had expressed toward her brother.

In fact, she seemed entirely at ease. Brushing a bit of fluff from her fingernail, she picked up the slender table knife from the tray and began to tool at the edge of it. "I can see you're surprised. Not every fae walks through shadows." She blew a puff of breath on the nail. "That's more of a Riven Court talent, and my mother was of the Storm Court."

Mireille attempted composure. "Is every fae of the Storm Court able to shift as you do?"

Nisha's dark eyes rose to Mireille in an unflattering

manner that reminded Mireille far too much of the prince. "Do you know nothing of the fae? Truly?"

"How would I?"

She lowered the utensil. "Are we to believe you are entirely unaware of the fae who glamour their way into Westrende?"

"No," Mireille said. "Indeed, I was aware of glamour. But those are human forms. Only a trick of the light." Mireille startled at the bark of laughter that escaped her companion. She took up her cup for a careful sip of tea, and a moment to think, before settling the cup back onto its saucer. "So, fae can alter their forms as well as use glamour."

Nisha leaned forward, gesturing loosely with the knife while she spoke. "You are from a royal family. You must understand power. Yet, you bargain yourself away to a prince and know nothing of his magic." She shook her head and speared the knife into a block of cheese.

Mireille's gaze drifted toward the knife. She found she did not like that it remained within reach. "It is not as if you make it easy. I have done nothing but search for knowledge of that very kind."

"In books?" Nisha scoffed. "In Rivenwilde's own library?" She eased back against her chair. "I thought better of you, Princess. Truly."

"Strange that you would think of me at all."

The corner of Nisha's lip rose slightly. "You are a princess, are you not? Perhaps with the aim of becoming a queen." Her tone made it clear she did not regard Mireille's title as it was, let alone the absurd notion she might become queen.

"The prince is your brother. Is your situation so dissimilar to mine?"

Nisha took up a pastry and tore it in half, but didn't eat it. "Fae titles are bestowed by the land, not the people. A prince of Rivenwilde may only ever be prince while his lands are torn apart. The boundary prevents his power from reaching past the walls. Why do you think the Rive was created in the first place? Why do you think we so badly want it down?"

Mireille fought to keep her expression neutral. Nisha had given her more answers in a moment's conversation than she and Thomas had been able to secure in days. The prince was caged, the Rive keeping his power in check. He could never be king while the boundary still stood, never access the full power of the land. While he had been trapped, the fae queen had been snatching up the surrounding lands, doing her best to steal and conquer. She had only grown in power, all while the prince was confined... and searching for a princess, one he did not seem to want to marry.

Mireille wondered what would happen if he ever got free. She wondered if it was already too late.

Nisha wrinkled her nose and dropped the pastry onto a plate without having taken a bite.

"What will happen when the Rive falls?" Mireille dared to ask.

Nisha's lips curled coyly. Mireille found she liked the woman much better as a mink. "Now, Princess, fae affairs are not within your purview. I would advise you to think twice before making such inquiries." As she stood, her gaze swept over Mireille. "I will leave you with one last morsel of advice. Whatever game you are trying to play in the Riven Court, you will lose. I suggest you play no games at all, particularly where my brother is concerned." Then the air shimmered and Nisha was once again animal. She turned, her sleek body gliding out of sight the way she had come.

Mireille stared at the space the fae had occupied, thoughts swimming. Every conversation since she'd arrived left her with more questions than answers. And answers were the reason she had come.

CHAPTER 8

Mireille's dinners with the prince had not gone as she had hoped. As he sat silent and stony at the far end of the long table, unreceptive to conversation, the time slipping away weighed on Mireille's every decision. If she could reclaim the moment they'd had in the ballroom, she might have a chance, but it seemed to have only served to fuel his determination to avoid her.

There had been no further mention of the incident in his quarters, though she had noticed when she'd changed for dinner that someone had removed her own paper knife and anything else pointy from her room.

She considered Nisha's warning about playing games. Such had never been her intention, but she supposed it was not so different than the games of any court. Except Mireille had no idea what the opposing party actually wanted. It was a considerable disadvantage.

Alder's every action made clear he had no intention of encouraging a wife. At the rate things were going, she suspected he might prefer she choose to break their bargain instead.

It felt impossible, and yet she could not surrender.

"Tell me about the marriage ceremony."

At her abrupt statement, Alder's gaze shot up to meet hers. Even across the distance, long table between them, his full attention made Mireille feel exposed. He said, "What matter are the details?"

She lowered her chin. "Should I not be concerned with the potentialities of my future?"

A muscle jumped in his neck beneath his high collar. It seemed she had hit another nerve. The man must be entirely made of nerves. "Any information you require will be provided before the ceremony." His attention returned to his plate, a clear dismissal.

She pursed her lips. If they were playing a game, she was losing. "About tonight, when I am sleeping—"

"I will see to it, as I've said."

Given that the *it* he referred to was her being puppeted by a fae queen's magic, Mireille found she could not so easily accept its dismissal. "Exactly how do you intend *to see to it?*"

She managed to keep her tone even, but the prince's fingers flexed where he held a fork. His dark eyes slowly lifted, pinning her to the spot. "If you wander, I will *see to it* that you are contained."

Mireille's lips parted. "Contained?"

He dropped his gaze. Again.

"Is there some part of you that truly believes I will let such a comment go unchallenged?"

"You will be protected."

"I am asking you how." She pressed her palms flat on the table, aware that she was not entirely gaining ground in her plans to melt the prince's heart. "Can you not imagine why I would be concerned with the details, what it is like to have your will stolen, to know that that any moment you might be walked through a window into the open night air and unable to stop it?" She shook her head. "You'll forgive me if your offer of containment is no great comfort."

When his gaze lifted again, it tracked her posture, her flushed cheeks, and his expression softened. His words, however, remained a disappointment. "You are protected. I will protect you. There is no further explanation I can offer."

She let out a light huff of laughter, spurring him where she might since he was not willing to give. "If you want to forgo sleep to watch my every movement, then so be it. At least Thomas will finally be allowed a night's rest."

MIREILLE LAY awake in the center of her massive bed, dreading midnight. The queen would come for her, the way she always did, but this time, the prince would be waiting. She told herself it couldn't be worse than what had happened in the prince's rooms, her own hand driving a blade toward her heart then the prince knocking her to the ground to hold her there, but she knew it wasn't true. It could be far, far worse.

Despite those fears and against her will, when the weight of the queen's magic drifted into the room, Mireille sank into sleep. Her last thoughts were that Thomas, who had refused to leave her room, would keep her safe. There was no need for Alder's protection. All would be well.

At first, she slept fitfully, hovering on the edge of wakefulness and plagued by scenes she could not quite grasp. Flashes of her mother, her father, memories from when she'd been only a girl. Then she dreamed of walking outside the Riven-wilde palace, in the lane bordered with orange trees. The soft scent tickled her throat, reminding her of the white blossom Alder had gifted her in a rare moment of kindness. But had it truly been kindness? She was trapped in an impossible position, and he seemed intent on keeping his secrets.

Dream Mireille studied the night-darkened blossoms, lamenting her fate, when a low whisper sounded in her ear. "My princess, things are not so unfortunate as you suppose. All you have suffered will be answered for, your every wish gratified."

She spun to face the source. It was a woman's voice, softly accented, and somehow an assurance. Nothing like the wicked queen. Then another voice, one like the prince's, a caress against her skin, though he was nowhere in sight. "Do not try to find me out, no matter how I may be disguised, for what you find will be your undoing."

In the dream, Mireille shot up in bed, a warning in the woman's voice echoing in her mind as true as the beat of her heart. "Do not trust your eyes. Do not let yourself be deceived." The words seemed to beg her to save the prince from cruel misery, shadows woven through every one.

The door to the prince's room was closed, but midnight was near. He would be listening on the other side, waiting for her to roam. Thomas stretched out on the floor in front of the main door, and furniture was blocking the hidden panel. She was safe, safer than she had been in a long while. So why did the pounding of her heart disagree?

Midnight had come, and Mireille had not risen from her bed.

Something was wrong, though. As the shadows cleared, the room felt suddenly eerie and unfamiliar. The entire space was lit with the dim glow of moonlight, too bright, as if the moon had lowered itself to peer through her window.

Thomas was not in his spot by the door, it was only a lump of fabric. Mireille's fingers curled into the bedding, only to release when she realized they were clad in soft gloves. She wore a sage gown, one that might have been appropriate in

Westrende were she playing the part of a proper princess in search of a husband.

Attention so thoroughly on her state of dress, Mireille startled when she became aware Alder had appeared beside her bed. She flinched back from his proffered hand, unsure if it was some new trick by the fae queen. The unnatural moonlight gilded his sharp features, his expression impassive, more like himself and less of the version that had appeared in her earlier dream.

"Mireille," he said, hand still extended.

Her eyes narrowed at the gentle way he said her name, but the fine line above his brow was plain to see. There was no indication that it was not truly the prince. He seemed so very tired.

Fighting the tremble in her fingers, she placed her gloved hand into his, then climbed from her bed, sliding her feet into silk slippers that matched the dress. Whatever was happening, she would soon find out.

Alder led her from the room, and she went with him silently. Had she wanted to question him, she was not certain she could. For the first time, the queen had not come for her. A fae prince had instead.

"How are you doing this?"

Mireille watched as Alder's long fingers traced the leaves of a wisteria tree, its trailing blooms quaking in the soft night breeze. He had led her there through a maze of gardens that surely would not be safe for her to journey alone. The unnatural glow of moonlight had followed, allowing her to see more clearly than true night might allow.

Alder brushed a purple blossom with the tip of a finger. "She can only reach you while you are sleeping because your subconscious is unoccupied. Here, however, I may influence you as well."

"And where is here?"

He didn't look at her. "In your dreams."

"Well, that is terrifically unsettling." She felt her brow furrow. "And while you are with me..."

"She is not."

So the prince must occupy her dreams to keep the queen at bay. *Contained*, he had said. She supposed it was preferable to anything else she might have imagined. But she wondered at the broken way she'd drifted at first, and how much of a battle it might have been.

"She cannot reach us here?"

"Not when I am present."

Mireille nodded, hoping it was true. "Then I must tell you."

He turned to her.

"It is not just I under the thrall of the queen. It began slowly, with messengers, courtiers, kitchen staff. Every night, citizens of Norcliffe fell under her spell. Every night, someone or something becomes a risk." She did not add, *to me*. She swallowed, hating the way the words tasted, hating that she was helpless to stop it. "The queen desires to end me and end my kingdom. I came here to find a way to save myself and to save Norcliffe. The truth of the matter is, we had nowhere else to turn."

Alder stared at her for a long moment, as if weighing her words. They were sincere, even if she had not told him everything, even if she *could* not.

He said, "I gave my vow. You are under my protection and will remain so as long as you remain inside these walls."

He did not offer to extend that protection to her kingdom, but she would take what she could get. She glanced at the surrounding garden, the wisteria tree at its center. If the entire court felt alive, the garden was its beating heart. Every bloom and leaf breathed with magic, their stems seeming to dance, pulsing with the power that was Rivenwilde. The power that lived through its prince. "Why bring me here?"

Transfixed by their surroundings, she again started when Alder gently gripped her wrist. He led her beneath the wisteria tree, only stopping at its base. Alder slid the glove from Mireille's hand, then guided it to trace the rough patterns of the ancient bark, another maze, but one to be walked with fingertips. Her heart thundered at his gentle touch, so much more real than anything she had felt in a dream before, then his touch was gone, leaving her to continue tracing the aged trunk alone. Warmth seeped into her fingertips, but she could not bring herself to draw them away. It was unquestionably fae magic, but not like she'd ever experienced before. The tree felt, impossibly, like Norcliffe.

Like home.

She released a breath, and the prince said, "The wisteria is a direct connection to one's kin." He was so close behind her that his chest brushed her shoulder, his words a feather against her ear. "You said you were worried about your family. All you must do is touch this tree, and you will know that they are well."

Mireille did not know if the prince was offering her a kindness or simply bowing to the rules of hospitality after she mentioned her unhappiness. But the tree felt so much of home, providing a sensation of comfort that, somehow, she truly believed her kingdom had not yet fallen.

"Does it please you?" He had shifted away from her, his words more distant.

"Yes," Mireille said, her palm against the tree, heart swelling with warmth. Norcliffe and her father were running out of time, she knew, in danger because of the very fae queen that Alder had believed Mireille had willingly allied with, the one who had followed her to Rivenwilde.

But while he might still be fae, Mireille could not fault him for what the queen had done. She began to turn, getting out only the word, "Thank—" before she gasped, sitting up in bed.

Thomas was stretched out on the floor before the main door, asleep. The doorway to the prince's chamber was sealed. Mireille swiped a gloveless palm across her forehead, then let out a shaky breath. It had only been a dream; she'd never left the bed at all. And yet, the memory of bark beneath her fingertips and Alder's whispered words lingered on her skin.

CHAPTER 9

Mireille spent the next morning peering out every window of the palace. If she could spot the purple of wisteria blossoms, or even the path they had taken to find it, then she could be certain the dream had been real. Never mind how real it felt, when the queen had come for her, it was always only to direct her actions. Alder had somehow reached Mireille more deeply, but he had not taken her thoughts or her will.

For his part, Thomas had slept the night through and could offer no additional clues. But the staff had been helpful in other areas of their search, revealing scraps of information regarding previous kings and queens and how they had been bound, so he hoped to gain more as the fae prepared for the week's events. She'd had to swear to Thomas that she would not leave the castle in search of proof before he left to seek out more members of the staff.

Deciding she might have better luck from a higher vantage, Mireille climbed a narrow flight of stairs at the end of the corridor. Her stomach sank when she crested the stairs only to find the double doors that she'd encountered the day before. She spun, certain it was not possible that the corridor where she stood connected to the staircase she'd used the previous day, but where the narrow stairwell that she had just climbed had been, was a different one—one she had not climbed. Mireille ran to the bottom, finding the entrance hall, its elaborate carvings seeming to peer down at her, more threatening than they had been before. Feet light on the marble floor, she ran toward the west wing until she was breathless, then took another stair to the next floor. The massive doors loomed in front of her once more. She ran again, to the third floor, and higher. But every staircase she topped, every corridor she turned, led her back to the throne room, as if the palace meant to send her a message.

Mireille stepped back, nearly falling on the top step of the grand staircase. A fae woman watched her from the hall, taking a bite of a small, misshapen apple. The wet crunch echoed through the space.

Abandoning entirely her plan to find the wisteria tree or any single thing on the upper floors, Mireille came down the staircase, striding past the fae woman without a word. At her back, laughter echoed over the marble. Mireille did not care.

Safely away long enough to catch her breath, her heart resuming its pulse, Mireille perched on a stone windowsill. The large glass pane revealed a flower garden, its bright blooms playing host to abundant butterflies. The sun was beginning to set, casting warm color across the greenery. It was a picturesque sight, but not one she had seen in the dream the night before.

A throat cleared behind her. Mireille turned, half dread at the prospect of another encounter with a fae, but it was only Noal.

Her shoulders relaxed, and she resumed her study of the garden's butterflies. "It is beautiful here. I quite regret not being able to explore the grounds and the kingdom farther."

"That is precisely why I've found you," Noal said. When her attention returned to him, he explained, "Because you cannot attend our festivals outside his protection, the prince would like Rivenwilde brought to you."

She eyed him skeptically. "This was the prince's request?"

Noal's lips parted. He smiled. "The actions of the palace staff reflect directly on the prince, Your Highness. Our job is to anticipate his wishes. All we do is at his request, in a manner of speaking."

THEY WALKED through several corridors that did not seem to shift, and Mireille resisted the urge to glance back to be certain they remained once she had passed. But when Noal led her into the courtyard, all her unease was forgotten. She gasped, and she could not be ashamed of it.

From the center of a massive archway draped in vining roses, their blooms as big as her outstretched hand, Mireille took in a scene that might have come out of a fanciful painting. Fae in colorful gowns danced among the foliage, playing games and acting out melodramas and enjoying general revelries. A small orchestra performed the most beautiful melody, and the scents of flowers and food filled the air. Sculptures rose through the greenery between a maze of pathways, colored ribbons strung from column to column, and laughter echoed from beyond the shrubbery where a picnic had been laid over the ground.

It was a delight. A festival on palace grounds.

"There you are," Nisha said, suddenly beside them. "What took so long? We had to start dancing without her."

"She was exploring the palace."

Noal's reply held no particular tone, but Nisha's attention shifted consideringly to Mireille. She took Mireille's arm. "Come, Princess. Let us introduce you to the best of the

Riven Court before my brother finds out. Do you sing, perchance?"

THAT EVENING, after Mireille had been returned to her room and had washed the fruit from her hands and paint from her cheeks, Noal appeared at her door.

"I suppose you are here to inform me of some pressing business of the prince, and that it would perhaps be best that I dine alone in my room?"

His chin dipped in acknowledgement. "The prince is indeed very busy and has sent me to inform you of such." No hint of the afternoon's festivities remained on his person, but something mischievous danced in his eyes. "I find, in fact, that I would be remiss in my duty should I not encourage you to avoid his highness's study at all costs."

"At all costs, you say?"

He laced his arms behind his back, rocking a bit on his heels. "Truly, the prince's study would be the last place he would want you to dine."

She narrowed her eyes. "Acting in anticipation of his wishes, I see." Mireille wasn't certain why Noal was making such attempts to bring her and the prince closer, but she could use all the help she could get, even if she didn't trust anything that brought joy to the expression of a fae.

"I am sure I do not know what you mean," he said.

Mireille nodded. "Very well. I agree it would be the height of presumption to invade the prince's study when he's in such great need of privacy. I thank you for your advice."

He inclined his head before turning to walk the corridor. Mireille thought she heard the echo of a whistled tune when he rounded the corner, but she was already up from her seat and on the way to her wardrobe to prepare. The prince had raised the stakes the night before, bringing her safety in her dreams. She needed to prove she was worth his efforts.

She needed to be certain he would let her in.

AT PRECISELY NINE, Mireille surprised Alder by knocking on his study door.

"Since you've been so reluctant to abandon your princely obligations, which is honorable, truly, I thought I should make it as effortless as possible for you to fulfill your duties as host." She strode past him into the room.

Alder stared at her, frozen in his place at the doorway. He made no mention of the dream, but she did not think he would, real or not. He had come to her in her bedchamber and imagined her a Westrende gown. Mireille suspected those were things a prince of Rivenwilde would not admit even upon the threat of death.

Safely inside and a good distance past, she turned to face him. "So, I will take dinner here, with you." Her tone brooked no argument, but he did appear as if he had one at the ready. Mireille smiled. "Alder."

His brow lowered. "Why do I imagine Noal will not need to be ordered to bring a second plate?"

"He is very clever, I'm certain he'll sort it out." She glanced around the room, looking for something, *anything* to redirect their conversation. She refused to let one more night go by without learning something useful or breaking down his walls. Her gaze caught on a stack of books atop a side table. "Do you read often?" The beginnings of a civil conversation, at the least, even if she felt a bit like a ninny asking in the middle of his personal library.

"When necessary."

Her gaze shot back to him, where he stood suddenly close. Not menacingly, exactly, but her pulse picked up a beat. She said, "Surely you enjoy at least some activities that aren't strictly necessary. Or do you only find satisfaction brooding alone in your dark study?"

A look of genuine surprise crossed his face. It did not last long. "I do not *brood*. I have never."

She had to bite down a smile. "Highness, I daresay it is one of your most finely honed talents."

"What would you know of my talents?"

He was baiting her, she knew it. She shrugged. "If you have any others, they have not been demonstrated thus far."

A noise came from deep within his throat. "And what talents have you to speak of?"

Mireille had sparred with nobles before, and she knew the prince was quick, but a long-buried ember lit in her at his smug expression. She found she would like very much to wipe it from, at the very least, those lips.

There was a talent she could show him, one of her finest, and though it bore a high price, the game she was attempting had even higher stakes. She lifted her chin, swallowing the familiar sensation of grief tickling her throat. "I will show you, if you like. But I cannot do it here."

There was no disguising the surprise that flitted across his features.

She would have given nearly anything for Noal to interrupt them with dinner that very moment and relieve her from a show of boldness, but the corridor outside the study remained stubbornly silent.

The tickle in her throat grew to a lump as Alder offered

his arm. Her hand nestled in the crook of his elbow, Alder gestured toward the door. "Lead the way."

His tone gave her courage. It was a dare, and if Mireille knew anything, it was that men on a gamble always had their tell.

SHE SAT at the piano she had discovered during their palace tour —the very one she had avoided. Gleaming instruments stood around them in silent witness, the blue and gold draperies nearly black in the moonlight. Looking down at the keys before her, Mireille took a shuddering breath. But Alder stood at her back, waiting, and she placed her fingers on the heavy ivory keys.

She could do it. It was only a simple song. She had done far more dangerous and daring things. Deciding on one she had played a hundred times before, she closed her eyes, but her fingers made a different choice.

Mireille nearly missed a note at the unexpected tune, one of the last songs she had played for her mother. It had been a favorite. But she did not falter, letting herself sink into the music, her fingers moving without thought, always just where they should be. The instrument was impeccable and her notes built to a devastating crescendo that echoed through the dark hall. She had needed this, she realized, so lost in the fae world with only Thomas to anchor her to everything she had left behind. She had needed the reminder of who she was, of what she had endured before and why it was so important to give her all. The song tapered off, its final notes a receding tide.

Swallowing back tears, she managed a casual, "There, do you still find me so talentless?"

When Alder did not reply, she looked back at him. He held her gaze, his dark eyes searching. He said not a word, but lifted his hand. She slid hers into it, their gazes locked. Moonlight cut a sharp line across his features, a stark reminder that he was wholly fae. But he only stood, keeping hold of her hand, his expression soft. She rose from the bench, her body seemingly drawn to his of its own will, her heart hammering in her throat. They were very close. They were very alone.

"Extraordinary," he breathed.

Her lips parted, and his eyes tracked the motion. Then, as if suddenly remembering himself, he turned and precisely tucked her hand into the crook of his arm.

Heat rose up Mireille's neck as he led her from the room without a word.

In the study, Noal and Kin hovered near a table perfecting two place settings.

Alder released Mireille from his arm, stiffly gesturing for her to enter. She no more than took a step inside, having given up discovering anything from the man after their encounter, when he cleared his throat, leaned in, and said, "I enjoy sculpture. And, it must be said, I am not terribly unskilled at it."

She spun to ask him more, but he was already disappearing down the corridor, leaving Mireille to dine alone.

She let him go.

Noal approached, his interest plain.

Forcing a smile, Mireille said, "I believe I will take my meal in my rooms after all." Eyes on the open doorway, she added, "But moving forward, this is where I will spend my evenings."

THOMAS EYED HER SKEPTICALLY. "He likes to *sculpt?*"

"Keep your voice down," she hissed, glancing at the sealed door into the prince's rooms, even though she doubted he was there.

Thomas whispered, "I don't see how we can use this."

"I will take anything at this point." If Alder could only soften to her, to open up a bit, she might feel able to reveal precisely what she needed.

Thomas lifted a brow. "Fortunately, I have learned something a little more helpful."

She sat forward. "Tell me."

"I persuaded Kin to attain a proper wardrobe for you."

Mireille glanced at the wardrobe, but her mind was on the sage green gown that Alder had, possibly, dreamed for her.

"But that is not the interesting part. Mid-undertaking, Kin hinted that the prince has bindings placed on him, and I do not mean by the existence of the Rive. Bindings separate from the curse, not on the land, but on the prince himself."

"Are you certain that was her meaning?"

"Yes, because she was vehemently reluctant to reveal more, and I believe it's connected to the fae queen herself."

"Our fae queen?"

"The very one. It must have something to do with why he accepts any willing princess into his kingdom. It cannot be a coincidence one queen is entangled with you both."

She straightened. "But that makes no sense. He cannot become king while the Rive stands. The boundary has him trapped. How would marrying a human princess change that?" If it could, he would have married long ago.

A hint of the confidence she hadn't seen in so long slid across Thomas's features. "Precisely. So what are the terms of the binding and how are they connected to the wedding bargain?"

Mireille stood to pace. Thomas was right. She should have been less worried about discovering their rules and law, and more worried about why the prince had agreed at all. "He said something about being forced to entertain the bargains. But if he has no true desire for a wife, why bring her into his home?"

Thomas leaned back into his chair.

The prince had vowed to protect Mireille. He had shared the wisteria tree. There must be a reason, something he stood to gain.

She just needed to discover what it was.

CHAPTER 10

The familiar weight of the fae queen's magic settled upon her once again and Mireille felt her body begin to rise from the bed. Then the heavy sensation suddenly disappeared, along with the sickly-sweet scent of hawthorn flower, and Mireille's eyes blinked open to the glow of unnatural moonlight that filled her room.

Alder stood over her, as if he'd been waiting.

Taking his proffered hand, Mireille swung her feet toward the edge of the bed, and realized the dress she wore was far different than the night before. Her free hand came up to the lace that curled at her neck, matching the butterfly sleeves and the lace that nearly covered her hands. It felt like... A wedding gown.

Had she conjured such a thing, or had it been him? Aghast, she met the prince's gaze, unsure which might be worse.

He made no comment, only turned to lead her from the room. They followed the same path as before, through the maze of gardens that surrounded the wisteria tree, but though her room was roughly the same in the dream as when awake, the corridors and paths never were.

The night air was warm, and fireflies danced amid the swaying greenery. In the distance, soft rain pattered against leaves. The gentle scent of wisteria clung to everything, its presence alone working to ease Mireille's distress. She said, "It is beautiful here."

Alder glanced down at her. "It is."

Mireille recalled that she had a purpose. No matter how seductive the idea of sinking into the peace the garden brought, she had to find her course. "Why do you wish to be free of it?" His brow lowered in confusion, and she asked, "Are these lands not enough for you?"

His lips tightened and it appeared he would not respond, then he turned abruptly to face her. "The land chooses its ruler. There is no *enough*. The land does not wish to be divided, and so I, as its prince, must find a way to unrend it, to destroy the curse that holds us within its walls."

She stepped closer, his figure in the moonlight somehow more imposing, yet he was not as icy and closed off as before. Mireille wasn't certain what had changed, but she had no interest in pretense. "What happens when the boundary falls? You will rise to king and the land will be satisfied? Or will it want more?" It was hard to imagine the Rive coming down as anything good, not when she had seen what an unbound queen was capable of. Part of her, a part she understood may not be entirely virtuous, wanted to keep them caged.

Alder's expression darkened. "You think me so power hungry?"

His tone sent a chill down her spine. Her shoulders drew back. It was only a dream. She would speak as she pleased. "You accepted my bargain with no apparent desire to have me as a wife. I was given to believe we would be wed, but it seems as if you only wish for me to break the bargain, so that you might add me to your collection of prisoners."

He stepped nearer. "What makes you think I have no intention of marrying you? Do you truly believe I would not honor my word?"

She craned her neck to look up at him. "You're evading the point. You have done nothing but attempt to keep distance between us. You want my choice to be a prisoner. Why else bring me to Lord Cadby and make clear that I would be choosing relative comfort? Why else not show me a single consideration above what is required by law of hospitality?"

He leaned in so that he looked her directly in the eye. "If being a prisoner of Rivenwilde sounds so preferable to being my wife, then perhaps your decision has already been made."

She released a growl of frustration. "Would you please cease answering my concerns with accusations."

The corner of his lips twisted in a manner that made Mireille uncomfortably aware of how churlish she was being. After a moment, he released a resigned breath. "I felt the fae queen's magic on you. That was why I agreed to the bargain. That is why I... held myself in reserve."

Mireille's own breath caught.

"I was not wrong," he added. "I will admit I never expected you to allow her into my home. But even before you entered my chambers, it was evident you had ties to her. As an ally, or a pawn, or a victim. I believed you the former."

The subtle swaying of the flora seemed to shift, as if agitated. Mireille asked, "And what is it that you believe now?"

He did not answer. It was answer enough. Alder believed she could be conspiring with the creature who had entirely destroyed her life. The one who had threatened her kingdom so thoroughly that she'd been left with no choice but to abandon her family and secure a bargain with a fae prince.

Her fists clenched tighter. "I am no ally or pawn, and though some have given it their best attempt, I am *no one's* victim. I have told you before, and I will say it again. Norcliffe is under threat. I stand before you now, in this—whatever this is—because of her."

He studied her face, then lifted a hand to pluck a leaf from her hair. She jolted when he reached toward her, and they both knew it. The bravado of her speech didn't change what a fae was capable of. But he was not the queen. He held the leaf for a moment between his fingertips, then let it fall to the ground.

He was using her as a tool to unbind his kingdom. She was using him to save her own. She could not have one without the other.

"Is any of this even real?" she asked.

"That depends how you define what is real. The garden is true, but we linger now in your dream. Your mind conjured the way your hair is styled, the gown you wear. Will it not persist in your memory? Does it not become part of your existence?"

Heat flushed her cheeks. The wedding gown certainly felt more significant knowing she was responsible for it. She would have somehow preferred it had been his conjuring. She said, "I suppose if it does not exist in the morning, then it is not truly real."

His fingers trailed across the lace covering her arm, and her traitorous body reacted to the touch, leaning nearer.

He said softly, "It feels real enough to me." But his gaze never met hers, instead shifting toward the moon in what was most certainly not a sky Mireille had imagined. "The midnight hour is far beyond us. Good night, Mireille."

She opened her mouth to protest, but darkness took her instead.

MIREILLE JOLTED; someone was standing over her where she lay in her bed. Her eyes flew open, her heart racing, but it was not the unnatural glow of a dream that lit her room, only lamplight.

Noal stared down at her, his dark eyes narrowed consideringly. He held a silver tray, its contents smelling of tea and freshly buttered toast. He said, "Forgive the intrusion but it's onto midday. If we were to wait any longer, you would not have time to prepare."

From his spot on the settee, Thomas lifted a toast point. "I told him to let you sleep."

She swiped a palm across her face. She could not remember ever lying in so long when she wasn't ill. She looked back to Noal. "And what am I to prepare for?"

"There's to be a ball," he explained. "Kin is here to assist you."

Mireille only then noticed the woman standing near the bathing chamber door. "So you were all three just... waiting for me to wake?"

Noal set the tray on a bedside table and gave her a meaningful look. "You'll need to be rested for what's to come."

When he quit the room, Mireille looked to Thomas, who only shrugged. "You know as much as I."

Kin frowned at them both, but made no effort to communicate additional information.

Mireille picked up a piece of toast, but her stomach turned, still haunted by the dream. The prince had thought she'd been in league with the queen and had still brought her into his home. For what, she didn't know. Perhaps to get closer to the queen. Perhaps something darker. Her gaze lifted to meet Thomas's, desperate to share what she had learned. But his gaze was on Kin. And Kin's was on Mireille's hand where it clutched her dressing gown.

A quarter hour later, Thomas was gone and Mireille was chin-deep in a hot bath, the prince's words running through her mind again and again. Kin placed a stack of towels and a jar of oil on the small table beside the tub. The door to the bathing chamber eased open and Kin absently lifted a foot to press it closed. Something low and dark wandered in, vaguely catlike, but before Mireille could even register it was not feline, the creature shifted to a woman around six feet tall. Kin fell back, knocking into the table and overturning its contents. Mireille darted up to help, slipped on the oil that had coated the tub edge, and splashed water across Kin and the floor. She cursed, wiping at her stinging eyes.

Nisha sneered down at both of them. In a simple cream gown that draped her body perfectly, she looked every bit a princess of fae, even if she had only moments before been a mink. The entire weight of her distaste turned on Mireille. "Why aren't you ready? I need time to work."

"You?" Mireille choked.

Nisha rolled her eyes, then made a gesture at Kin. "Get her dried off." She gave Kin a full once-over and shook her head. "The both of you." With a flick of her skirts, she strode out of the bathing chamber, making a feline-like huff of disgust.

Mireille locked gazes with Kin. Whatever was happening with the ball, it seemed Mireille was not the only one uninformed.

A quarter hour later, Mireille sat before a vanity table and small gilt-trimmed mirror, her silk dressing gown decorated with a delicate pattern of swirling vines and flowers. Kin ran a brush through Mireille's long locks as three fae women in simple staff garb looked on. One held a comb and assorted hair pins, another a sewing kit, and the third was apparently in charge of gowns.

Nisha snapped her slender fingers, then pointed at the gowns. The woman rushed to grab the first where it had been draped over a rack, then held it forward for Mireille's inspection. She repeated the process twice more, each of the gowns deep cerulean and soft, supple fabric, but varying styles.

Nisha said into her ear, "It's his favorite color." She backed away and gave Mireille an appraising but somewhat disappointed look. "I'm not certain it will suit your hair. How do you feel about feathers? No? Understandable." She patted her shoulder. "We will figure something out."

In the end, Mireille was forced to try on all three gowns, and the group eventually settled on one sewn of the softest silk, with a high neck and detailed with delicate vines in a slightly darker shade of blue. The same vines crawled down the sleeves of the dress, ending in embroidered foliage near the wrists. It was a fae gown, through and through. Mireille had never worn anything like it, but even Kin nodded her approval.

The dress was removed, adjustments made, and Mireille was bustled back to the vanity where her hair was pinned and twisted into an elaborate form. Mireille met Nisha's gaze in the curved mirror. "Are you going to tell me what you're up to?"

Nisha's grin was wicked. "If anyone knows how to truly tempt a fae male, it is me." She held a palm out, and the woman with the hair pins handed another over.

"Why would I need to temp a fae?"

Kin dusted color onto Mireille's cheek, distinctly not meeting her eyes.

"And why are all of you conspiring against him?"

Nisha made a sound in her throat, not unlike the dismissive sound her brother favored. "Careful, princess, for you're making it sound as if falling for you might be to his detriment."

Mireille caught the gleam in Nisha's eyes, but Kin's fingers trembled as she applied lotions and creams. The two seemed to be working toward the same goal but, possibly, possessed entirely different motivations. Nisha, Mireille thought, was giving her the appraisal of someone taking pride in their well-trained pet.

"There," she said. "Just one final touch." And Mireille was dabbed with the light, fresh scent of orange oil.

CHAPTER 11

Nisha and the fae ladies departed, and Thomas was finally returned to Mireille. He slid his hands into his pockets and stared openly at what they had done. "Well," he said. "That's quite a statement."

She raised a hand to her hair, delicate gold vines woven through, and lifted a softly curled tress away from her face. "I look like a queen."

"No question."

"It's the prince's favorite color, apparently."

"Solid choice."

She fiddled with the accents on the high neck of the gown. "Should we leap out a window and run for the hills?"

He grinned. "Probably. But you know how I love a ball."

Thomas did not love a ball, particularly, she suspected, not a fae one. "Quite," she said. She drew a deep breath. "So, we stay for you."

He raised a hand to his chest. "I am grateful, as ever."

She shrugged, the bulk of the gown shifting around her. "Least I can do."

His grin shifted into something more genuine. "Indeed."

They turned in unison at a knock on the door, and Mireille called for Noal to enter, as it was all she could expect, given that Nisha would never deign to knock. But it was Alder who stood on her threshold.

He was dressed in black, the fabric of his coat embroidered with silver thread shaped into thin, twisting branches. If her gown was the color of the sky in deep spring, his clothing was like night the heart of winter, the effect only emphasized by the sharp bone crown atop his dark hair. His eyes stayed on her for a heartbeat longer than was generally considered proper in polite society. Wordlessly, he offered her his arm.

Mireille cast a glance at Thomas, who gave her a firm nod. "I will be waiting right here."

She returned the nod, then slid her arm through Alder's, his warm, crisp scent sending a strange sensation through her belly. The prince did not acknowledge Thomas's vow, only led her from the room. They traversed a long corridor in tense silence. Mireille had overheard the prince make his own vow, telling Noal that she would attend no fae event lest she be on his arm, but she was not certain why he'd chosen to bring her at all. Perhaps, she thought, he was only afraid she'd show up unannounced mid-ball to surprise him for dinner.

Something shifted in an alcove, catching Mireille's attention. She kept her face forward but could not help but smile. It was Kin, likely waiting to meet Thomas. She could not begrudge the pair for not attending; they would probably have a much more agreeable time searching out clues to fae bargains than being shuffled on a gameboard by the likes of Alder and Nisha.

When they passed no one else in the corridor, Mireille's nerves got the better of her. "Are there any particular customs

I should know to observe? Will there be formal introductions?"

The question seemed to make Alder uncomfortable, though his stride did not falter. "It is simply a ball. You need only eat, if you like, and dance."

"Dance with you?"

His expression tightened.

"It's only that I was under the impression you wished me to stay away from fae gatherings."

"You have made clear you will read hidden intentions in my every action. Attend any such gatherings if you wish."

She doubted that meant he would not be right at her side, but she didn't argue, because they had reached the ballroom. Two fae men in long-tailed suits opened a set of double doors and the abrupt chaos of music and conversation filled the corridor.

"The doors are enchanted," Alder explained. "Guests enter through the main hall to lights and decoration, to encourage joyous celebrations."

"Wouldn't want such a thing echoing through the palace," she murmured.

He hummed in agreement, evidently missing her point. Alder guided her inside. Fae in fine silks, lace, and jewels swept gracefully across the marble floor, in perfect time with the music. Their wardrobes were far more elaborate than she might have guessed, their number overwhelming. Glittering chandeliers and tabletop candles shone golden light over the entire affair. It was warm and lively and distressingly unlike any ball she had attended before.

Alder glanced down at her, and she realized her grip on his arm was a little too tight. Curious glances followed their movement across the floor as he led her toward an impossibly long table bedecked with every type of sweet and sustenance imaginable. Alder released her arm to lift two long-stemmed glasses filled with something pink and sparkling, but his eyes were not on his task, instead scanning the ballroom, which seemed strange given that they'd just arrived.

No one dared approach, despite the throng, and there was something very urgent and wary about his look, sentiments she did not normally associate with the prince. She surveyed the crowd as well, but other than the entire hall being filled with powerful and potentially dangerous fae, found nothing that seemed amiss.

A moment later, as she lifted the glass to her lips, Mireille had her answer. A shiver seemed to go through every fae in the room. The crowd turned toward the main entrance. The double doors swung outward, revealing the fae queen of Mireille's nightmares. Maeve.

She was in the one place she should not be. The one place Mireille had thought herself safe.

Mireille took a step back and bumped into Alder. His hand slid over the small of her back, holding her in place.

Across the ballroom, Queen Maeve's sinister gaze fell upon Mireille, then lowered to Alder's steadying hand. Long auburn hair fell in glistening waves over the queen's gown, the flowing fabric glimmering in the light and sliding over her tall form like a living thing. "Bow," she commanded.

Every fae in the room except Alder dropped into a bow, the music cutting off with a clatter. Beside Mireille, the prince stood tall, anger radiating from him more like ice than fire. Maeve's laughter was the tinkle of bells. "Rise. For I am a guest, here to enjoy the festivities." She lifted her hand, and with it, the fae moved as one, rising awkwardly to face her.

There was no question they had moved by her hand, her magic, like the way Alder had frozen the dining room when Mireille had been attacked.

The queen's gaze met Alder's. She said, "I was invited by your prince, after all."

Mireille went cold. She made to run, certain she'd been snared, but Alder's touch had turned into a grip. There was no escape. Murmurs slid through the crowd, but Maeve gestured, and the music started up once more. Fae parted around her like the tides as she glided across the room. Her vibrant green eyes danced with amusement as she approached. "Prince," she said, no disguise to her pleasure. "I might have been insulted by the last-minute invitation, but it seems even your court was unaware of the ball until quite recently."

Alder was rigid, more so than any statue in the palace, and just as imposing as the day Mireille had met him. He said, "These are my lands. Here, we do as I wish."

Maeve inclined her head, a smile playing across her lips. Beyond them, the fae danced cautiously, their liveliness from earlier gone. The queen said coyly, "And would you wish to offer your guest a dance?"

The queen extended an arm, clad in a long silver glove, and Mireille tensed, every part of her wanting to jerk away. But Alder held her firm.

He said, "As you can see, my arm is already taken."

Maeve's bright eyes slid to Mireille. "Why, yes, Princess Mireille." She drew a fan from thin air, snapping it open in clear insult. Given the power she'd just displayed, it was unforgivably petty. "What a surprise to find you so far from home. Have you left your dear father?" She clicked her tongue. "I do worry about the poor man. Let us hope he fares well without you."

Heat flared through Mireille. She drew herself up, wanting nothing more than to strike the woman with that cursed fan, and possibly Alder, too. She had come to find protection, he had made a vow, and there stood the queen, invited by Alder himself and delivering barely veiled threats. "The kingdom of Norcliffe's fate does not rest on my shoulders alone."

Maeve lifted a brow meaningfully at Mireille's slender shoulders. "I should hope not."

In that moment, had she a weapon, Mireille could not have been trusted not to use it.

Alder shifted, the first he'd moved since the queen arrived, and Mireille's gaze flicked to him. "If you will excuse us," he told the queen, "I owe my betrothed a dance."

Maeve's expression remained unchanged, but her fury was a tangible thing that bit at the air around them. It felt as dangerous as standing in a lightning storm, and Mireille was a good deal certain one of them was about to meet their end, but Alder only swept past, pressing Mireille forward and toward the dance floor, with himself bewteen her and the queen. He took the drink from Mireille's hand, which she had quite forgotten she was holding but now bubbled thick and black, and deposited it on the tray of a passing server.

Then his hand was in hers, the other positioned at her waist, and he was leading her through the steps of an unfamiliar dance. Her cheeks were hot, her chest was tight, and hundreds of fae swirled around them in a dizzying blur.

"You are angry," he said.

She found focus, narrowing her gaze on his and stilling her trembling limbs. "Livid."

He drew her body tighter to his.

"How could you?" she hissed. "I told you what she has done. You understood that I was here for your protection, that my kingdom, my father, everything I hold dear is in danger from *her*."

His movements were steady and sure as he spun them in another turn, as if the entire world was not spinning out of control around them. "I had to be certain."

"Certain of what?"

He met her gaze.

"Certain that I was not her ally? That I was not here on her behalf?" She felt sick. "If I am a pawn in anyone's game, it is yours. I was a fool to trust you. And what care you for my allegiances? Why claim me as your betrothed?"

His eyes darkened. "You never trusted me." The music changed and Alder brought their dance to a stop in the center of the ballroom, his hand firm on her waist. He leaned forward, his breath hot on her cheek. He was very tall, and very imposing, and there was so very much of him right there in her space. "Maeve is gathering power. She has come for your lands. What makes you think she would not come for mine? The stakes are higher than you can understand. I had to be certain."

"Our enemy is the same. You knew all along."

"You have not been honest."

She glared back at him. "Nor have you. And not even solely with me. Your staff has done nothing but push us together, while even they are left in the dark. The curse you speak of is the Rive, but there is a binding on you that is more personal still."

His expression hardened. He did not like that she'd found out, that much was clear. She said, "You have done everything in your power to drive me away. Why do they encourage you closer?"

Around them, the dancing fae began to take notice of their scene. Alder leaned near, his lips brushing the shell of her ear. "They do not know everything."

She wasn't certain it was a confession, but across the room, drink in hand and ire simmering for all to see, Maeve watched with a strange tilt to her head. Mireille held the woman's gaze, lifting onto her toes to whisper into Alder's ear, her hand pressed to his broad chest. A spark of something hot shot through her at his closeness, and she was unsure whether it was fear, or something worse. "We need to move this discussion somewhere private."

The look he gave her was pure heat and, again, Mireille was unsure exactly how to process it. But the hand at her waist spun her to his side, and before she could summon even a second thought, she was ushered from the room.

CHAPTER 12

They stood alone in the night-darkened music room, and Mireille had to force her gaze away from the piano. There was a part of her that could not believe she had actually played for him. She wasn't certain what had come over her since she'd agreed to a bargain with a fae prince. Desperation, that was all.

Alder peered down at her, his face half in shadow and half in moonlight. He had let go his hold but had not stepped away. "What do you know of my bindings?"

The words were emotionless, but Mireille flinched nonetheless. "You need a princess to bring down the Rive."

He felt more dangerous in the moonlight, but when his words came, they were not in the tone he'd used before. If anything, they seemed pained. "I do need a princess."

"But not me. Why? What is it that I cannot offer you?" He turned away, and her hands balled into fists. "This is absurd. You said yourself we have a common enemy, and she's out there, right now, in your own ballroom."

Alder's shoulders sagged, a weight like the one she'd watched her father carry for years. He said, "It must be a princess of Westrende. The Rive split the land, but we are bound still. Our kingdoms can only be united with a union of the two."

After a moment, he turned to face her. "There is more, but I am bound from discussing the details." He pressed a palm to his chest, one of his long fingers tapping slowly over his heart. "Suffice it to say, a match of convenience would do me no good."

A very unpleasant sensation danced in Mireille's belly, writhing dread and nervous energy, and a strange sort of anticipation. She began to pace. "Then you refuse me because you are certain I cannot break it. Yet, you agreed to entertain the offer because you are required. And as a fae, you cannot break your vow, so your wish must be that I will terminate our agreement before the ceremony. You must have some plan in place, some way to prevent it, otherwise you would have been wed by now." Pacing ceased, she turned toward him, slowly lifting a hand to her collar. "Except, that choice surely belongs to me."

His eyes narrowed. "You would trap me in a curse? Knowing what that means?"

She shrugged. "Why, who's to say I would not prefer a life at court? What if I spirit my father away and we let her have Norcliffe?" It was evident that much, at least, he did not believe her capable of. Her voice dropped. "The queen has threatened my kingdom. I am my father's heir. If she is to take control, she will need me dead."

"Or married to a prince from another kingdom."

The terrible sensations inside her belly flipped. "Yes, or that. I would become queen of my husband's kingdom and would relinquish my claim to Norcliffe." And she could never become queen of Rivenwilde if the Rive held.

He asked, "Whose decision was it to bargain you to me?"

"Mine. Maeve had no hand in this. We would not have

been fool enough to trust anything we had not devised ourselves, not after she infiltrated the council and the royal advisors. I knew no one could protect me from a fae queen but a fae from another court. And the only place I might find a way to beat her was within your court, your library, your home. I had connections to Westrende—" She swallowed. "Friends who knew of the fae. But even then..."

"Your options were few."

She nodded, but guilt and shame had her glancing toward the window as she did. "There was nothing noble about it."

He was suddenly close behind her.

"Am I to understand you planned to find a way to defeat her first? That you hoped to never have to marry me?"

She forced herself to look at him. "I would do anything to save my kingdom."

"And to turn the Riven Court against your enemy queen?"

Mireille hesitated. She had not thought that far ahead. Throwing herself to Rivenwilde had been an act of desperation, likely a fool's errand that would only buy more time. She supposed she never believed, truly, that she could overcome the queen. But Norcliffe was worth the risk. "Yes. Whatever it took. Even that."

His chin dipped. "I will not pretend any of this was done for the safety of your kingdom, only mine. But I spoke the truth. Our enemy is the same. And I have every intention of besting her."

Mireille's lips parted. "Are you suggesting a truce?"

"Agree not to marry me. We will find a way to defeat her before the next moon."

The breath that huffed out of her may have sounded like a laugh. It was not. "I will agree to ally with you. Until then." She held a hand forward to seal the agreement and Alder took it. They stood, studying one another, the unlikeliest of partners, hand in hand.

A distant scream sounded, reverberating off the music room walls, and Alder's hand pulled from hers. He ran and it was all Mireille could do to catch up.

When he realized Mireille was chasing after him, he came back to her, a firm grip on her arms. "Stay far away from this. Find a room to hide in and lock the door. If you are in danger, just speak my name."

"But—"

Another scream sounded and Alder pressed her a step back. "Go. If you call me, I will come." He released her and rushed away.

He was right, and she knew it. Mireille had no power to fight against the fae. She hurried in the opposite direction, searching for a place to hide. As before, the palace layout seemed to shift, and she was not certain which way to run. But a landing of narrow stone steps led upward, and the scream had echoed from the lower floor.

Lifting her skirts to her knees, she sped to the higher level and down another long corridor. She gripped the lever of the door at the end of the corridor, but it would not turn. Words were carved into the wood in a language in which Mireille was not fluent, something about balance being kept—or possibly paid. Another distant scream rang through the palace and she moved to release the lever, but something sparked through her palm. Her hand yanked back, and the door creaked inward. When footfalls sounded on the stairs, Mireille hurried inside.

The moment the door swung shut behind her, she knew she'd made a mistake.

The only light in the room came from its center, the same unnatural glow of her moonlit dreams. But it was not a dream. She was awake, the floor solid beneath her feet, and before her stood an hourglass atop a table that was nearly as tall as her. The room smelled of hawthorn flower, thick, and sticky, and sweet. Dread rose through her, every fiber of her being begging her to step away, but Mireille's slippered feet drew her forward.

Roots grew through the floorboards, winding and tangling into one large mass that held the hourglass. Cradled by hawthorn branches, twisted into unnatural shapes and studded with dagger-like thorns, the glass seeped familiar magic, the magic Mireille had felt settling over her room every night the fae queen had come.

As she watched, a single glowing grain of sand dropped slowly through the narrow waist, as if settling in a sea. There was far more at the bottom of the glass than the top, though with the rate it fell she wagered it had been there a *very* long time. She reached one trembling hand forward but stopped short of touching it.

The fae queen's magic was emanating from an hourglass inside Alder's palace, as if the magic had intertwined with that of Rivenwilde. Mireille stepped back. The room was empty, other than the timepiece. The entire space seemed ancient and untouched. Perhaps as old as the Rive.

A common enemy, he had said. From a queen determined to gather lands. For the first time, Mireille wondered if Alder had more to lose than even she.

He would not want her there, she was sure of it. He would not want her to even know. She crept toward the door, keeping an eye on the table, then listened for any movement outside. The screams had gone silent. Mireille escaped into the corridor and hurried back in the direction she had come.

As she neared the foot of the stairs, she caught sight of Thomas running through a crossing corridor. She hissed out his name and he backtracked, peering up at her.

"I've been looking everywhere for you!" He reached out a hand. "Shadow creatures have attacked the ball. Let's get you back to your room."

She took the last few steps two at a time, then grasped his hand. "How did you know where to search?"

"Kin and I were in the library when the creatures attacked. We found a member of staff who saw you leave with Alder, before he came back alone."

As he tugged her along, Mireille could not bring herself to share what Alder had revealed. That he believed he'd taken an ally of his enemy into his court was proof enough that he was desperate. But the sand, well that proved that Mireille was not the only who was running out of time.

ALDER DID NOT COME to her room, and late into the night, Mireille finally climbed into bed. There was no way to know if the queen would find her, if the prince would intervene, or if the queen, so close, could overpower his will. Surely, he would not have invited such a danger into his own palace, but he was fae. There were no guarantees.

Thomas was in his post by the door, lying on his back, a hand behind his head and boots crossed at the ankle. The door to her room was locked. But as midnight neared, it was the prince's magic that settled heavily around her.

She sensed his presence, and the rich smell of bergamot, and opened her eyes.

Alder stood over her, offering his hand. When he helped her from the bed, her gown was revealed to be the deepest black. She was unsure if it was a gown of mourning, or simply that her slumbering imaginings had wanted to match the prince. She looked up at him.

He said, "I have a plan."

CHAPTER 13

Mireille reluctantly withdrew her hand from the wisteria tree. Norcliffe was well enough for the time being, particularly given that the queen was in Rivenwilde, and though the tree gave her comfort, she could not afford to linger. She turned back to Alder, his tall form limned in the strange moonlight. He no longer seemed quite so imposing, but she could not say whether that was owing to the dream, or that she knew his secret.

He had ambushed her with the queen's presence at the ball, but each night, he'd given her the gift of knowing her father was safe, and that Norcliffe still stood. She asked, "You said you have a plan?"

He stepped forward, his dark eyes searching her face. "It will require your cooperation."

"You want me to agree blindly when the last move you made was to invite my mortal enemy to dance alongside us. I may have agreed to an alliance, but I will not hand you indiscriminate trust."

His mouth tightened. "Because you believe me a monster

out to conquer human lands. Yet you would expect me to trust you when you would do the same as I."

"The same? I hardly think—"

He took another step forward. "I would do anything to protect my people."

Well, he had her there. She folded her hands neatly at her waist. Around them, the garden swayed in an imagined breeze. There was something calming about the rhythm, though, and Mireille tried to steady herself in its pace. She said, "You witnessed our encounter, besides that she sent me every night to walk to my death—" Her eyes shot up to meet his. "She drew me into your chamber, but given the chance, she chose to drive the blade into me." Not Alder, the prince who she had somehow bound.

"It was not the first time."

"She sends women into your chambers?"

His expression shifted. "No, that's—" He shook his head. "She merely taunts me. In my cage."

"Oh."

He stepped closer, and she shifted, too, her body reacting as if they were still in a dance. "Not an ally," he said. "Not a pawn." His last words were barely above a whisper. "But no victim."

One corner of her mouth ticked up. She couldn't help it. "Not a monster, not a conqueror, but not..." The hourglass rose again in her thoughts, and she could not say the words. Alder was trapped. He was bound by the Rive and bound by the queen and her curse. But he was still a fae.

He watched, waiting for her to finish, but when she did not, his shoulders relaxed and he moved to place his hand on either side of her waist.

"And what of this plan?" she asked against his chest, staring at the spot his finger had tapped during his confession.

He released a breath, then turned her with him to walk from beneath the wisteria and down a narrow path. Ancient stone pillars rose through the greenery, less alive than the ones in the palace, and Mireille wondered if they belonged to her memory or Alder's. He said, "The creature that attacked you on that first night was a miscalculation by my sister."

Mireille tensed, ready to pull away from him, but his next words stopped her short.

"The creatures let loose tonight were a miscalculation by the queen."

"Miscalculation?"

He kept his eyes forward. "Nisha wanted to be rid of you. She believed I had made the bargain against my will, like the others. That it would prevent the breaking of the Rive."

Mireille wondered how many times she had been watched unaware, not giving second thought to the many open windows and balconies that could be concealing a small dark mink. "She no longer seems to feel that way."

Alder's laugh surprised her. "No, I fear she does not. She's impulsive, sometimes recklessly so, but after a time, she believed our arrangement could come to benefit her."

"Has she confessed all this?"

His voice darkened. "She has not. But her schemes are transparent. She cares very little for covering her tracks. And any other fae would not have sent a message merely meant to frighten you off."

Mireille tried not to think about what the *merely* meant, but she knew enough of the fae to understand the gravity of her situation.

Alder paused before at a bench beneath a trellis of climbing roses, gesturing for her to sit. When she did, he settled beside her, the space small and quiet, and shaded from the dreamlight's glow. "Nisha's motives are not difficult to guess. If I were to marry anyone not from Westrende, the only way to bring down the Rive would be to bring down me."

If he married Mireille, his life and his kingdom would be at risk, the same as she. And yet, they were tied by the threat of a ruthless queen. "I still cannot reconcile your choice to invite the queen in. It seems a great deal of risk only to confirm her intentions and mine."

"That was not why she was invited." His tone was off, his attention on the moon through the canopy of leaves. "Tonight, once we returned to the ball, I intended to announce our betrothal to the court. She needed to be present. She will remain as guest and as witness."

Mireille stood abruptly, nearly knocking into him. "I did not agree to this." In fact, she'd agreed *not* to agree to the ceremony at all.

He gave her a speaking glance.

"This is your plan? To announce we've settled on giving up our kingdoms?" She paced only steps away, then immediately back. "You called me your betrothed to the queen. So you invited her to, what, test me first? Before the announcement? To test her?" She resumed her place on the bench. He did not shift over, only watched as she worked it out. "Because if we were to marry, I would be forfeiting my right as heir. You think she would no longer have reason to do away with me, that she would simply take Norcliffe and be on her merry way. But Rivenwilde would still be bound and under threat."

"It is more complicated than that."

He had no idea. But Mireille did not say so, she could not and still have any chance of coming out of the ordeal alive.

"I need Maeve to believe we intend to go through with the marriage, need her to act. That is what I needed to be certain of—that she will make an attempt before the turn of the moon." He leaned back. "And when she does, I will be ready for her."

"So we are to feint, to... pretend a marriage."

"Right up until the ceremony."

She watched him for a very long moment. "And I? What do I stand to gain from this?"

His expression was grim. "This is the price for breaking your bargain. Aid in my scheme and you will be free."

If the queen could be defeated, Mireille could return to Norcliffe. Their kingdoms could be saved. But how was she to believe he could do it?

"What if I do not trust that you can overcome her?" The marshal's words echoed through Mireille's mind. The price of breaking a bargain with the fae was always one too costly. No one would give it willingly. It had to be a trick. Escaping could not be so easy.

"That is the price you must pay."

She blinked. "You planned this from the start."

"I had considered my options. It could have gone other ways."

"Indeed," Mireille whispered. "For I was not even the first princess to agree."

His expression went hard. She did not care. She was not the only princess under threat by the queen, she was simply the last who had managed her way into his palace. There were more, surely, perhaps in the wing with Lord Cadby. Perhaps many more. It was apparent that her wince did not go unnoticed. Every moment, the possibility of preserving her kingdom felt further away. She said, "Then I have no choice at all. The only way to save Norcliffe is to agree to your ruse."

He leaned closer, voice low. "Had you another choice, would you take it?"

She bit back her initial response, because of course the safety of her kingdom, freedom for herself, and the defeat of the fae queen would be worth it. But it seemed unlikely that he would see it done. After all, he hadn't in all the time he'd spent cursed. The boundary wall was ancient, just like the Rive. No one had yet restored it. "I prefer to be told why and how our engagement will force her to act."

"As I've said, I am unable to reveal details. But know that my history with her is long, and you and I are not the only ones with something to lose."

She drew a shuddering breath. If she could not have his confession, then she would not give him hers. They would merely have to work together, doing all they could do drive the wicked queen off a cliff of her own making.

"Then let us bring her down, once and for all,"—she gave him her gaze— "husband."

<h1 style="text-align:center">CHAPTER 14</h1>

When Mireille opened her eyes, it was not to a moonlit canopy of leaves. It was to Thomas, staring down at her with a perplexed expression.

She groaned and rolled to her side. "Why must everyone suddenly stand over me in my sleep?"

"You are sleeping half the morning away, that is why." He poked her shoulder. "Tell me, for the household will not."

Mireille pressed her eyes closed very tight. She did not want to know what Thomas had heard. She did, however, have a very good idea. And it was a problem, because she'd vowed—been forced to vow—not to tell Thomas, or anyone else, of the prince's plan. And the prince's plan was very different from the one Thomas and Mireille had arrived with. "What do you mean?"

He spoke slowly, carefully enunciating each word. "Engaged to be wed."

She drew the blanket over her head.

"It was my understanding that you could barely tolerate him. And yet, one night, one dance, and the entire palace has

153

practically broken into song. They're hanging decorations, I hope you know that."

She mumbled a reply under her breath and could feel Thomas lean in. "What was that?" he said. "Didn't quite hear you, what with all the cowering in shame."

Mireille flipped the blankets down. "I said it wasn't only one dance."

The shock that crossed Thomas's expression was not put on. He rocked back onto his heels, ran a palm over his chest. "So, it's true."

"The prince and I have come to an understanding. It seems, unfortunately, that this is our best course of action."

He sank down on the bed and then, abruptly, appeared to recall she was no longer merely his friend. She was betrothed to another man. A fae prince. He stood, sidling awkwardly toward the foot of the bed. "What happened between last night and this morning to change your mind?"

She pressed up on the massive pile of pillows. "Honestly, Thomas, I told you about the dreams."

"Yes," he drew out the word. "And what, precisely, happened in last night's dream to alter your course so thoroughly?"

She could not tell him the truth. Not because he could not be trusted, but because Alder had told her that the only place that was truly safe to speak of secrets was in her dreams. They could not allow their plan to be foiled. It was too great a risk.

Guilt twisted inside her. But it would not be forever. Thomas would understand everything soon. Whether they managed it, or not. "He convinced me. We share a common goal. We both care about our people. And once she sees we are to be wed, the queen will turn her attention elsewhere."

Thomas's brow pinched. "Will she? Or will she go after your father?" He crossed his arms. "And Alder? What about him? What does a prince stand to gain when he doesn't even know—"

She cut him off with a raised hand. "That is enough, Lord Holden. I've made my choice."

He slid his hands into his pockets. "I see. Very well, then."

It felt horrible. Cruel. Unconscionable. She was definitely going to live with regret for eternity.

He said, "What shall I do today? For the cause."

She swallowed against the shaky feeling in her throat. "The engagement was meant to be announced last night, but the ball was cut short. It will be announced instead at a formal gathering this afternoon."

"Last night," he repeated. "Before your dream walk."

She stood. "I'll need to get dressed for the gathering. You're welcome to attend. If you'd like." She crossed to the bathing chamber, then closed the door behind her, bracing against it to catch her breath. Through the finely carved wood, she heard Thomas wait for her to take it all back, to tell him the truth, and then, she heard him leave.

Kin, evidently assigned as a lady's maid to assist Mireille before the event, came later. Mireille did not mind the company. After pinning her hair, Kin held forward a gown of jet-black silk. Mireille smoothed a finger across the silver embroidery of wicked bare branches, likely a match for the coat Alder would wear. It was not a gown suited for the balls of Westrende, but one only fit for a fae court.

Kin frowned and Mireille clumsily signed, *What troubles you?* The woman looked a bit as if she'd swallowed a small poisonous toad.

Do you love him? Kin signed back.

Mireille suddenly felt as if she had swallowed a similar, if larger and more lethal, toad. Thomas had not been exaggerating, then. The entire household must have been abuzz. And her concern was that the prince was *loved*.

Mireille could not recall the sign for *engagement*, so she replied, *I have chosen willingly.* It may not have been the answer Kin wanted, but it would have to do. Alder was exasperating, brooding, and stubborn. But he had kept his word. He had protected her. It was all she had.

It should not matter if her stomach grew alight when he stood too close. It should be of no consequence if she imagined, even for a moment, that he saw through everything to who Mireille really was. He considered it an arrangement only. There would never be more, because... well, because to him, it wasn't real.

She cleared her throat, returning her attention to the dress and its laced bodice. "Help me, will you?" Kin might ask of love and things uncomfortable to consider, but answering those questions was preferable to lying to Thomas, who was far more likely to accuse her of being rash or foolish. Because she was. Not as a rule, but certainly of late.

Kin kept her eyes lowered, attention pointedly on task, apparently dissatisfied with Mireille's reply. Or perhaps she was unable to convey what she wished for reasons of loyalty or magic, bound by the same rules as Alder. By the time Mireille had slipped on the long black gloves, she could take it no longer. She ducked forward, meeting Kin's gaze before signing. *Do you not trust in your prince to choose correctly?*

Kin's dark eyes were steady, but Mireille could not guess at precisely why. A knock sounded at the door, and Kin turned to answer it.

Noal, dressed in matching black with a white cravat tied so firmly against his olive skin that she wondered if he could properly breathe, studied her. "You look well."

"For a human about to dine with a fae queen intent on her murder, you mean?" She adjusted her gloves. "I am under the prince's protection, am I not? Is there any reason for concern?"

According to the prince, Noal was unaware of his plot, but the look in the man's eyes said he understood far more than he let on. He inclined his head. "I am to escort you to the study."

"I am ready," she said, though she was most certainly not.

Then Thomas came through the door in a manner that might fairly be called *bursting in*, before stopping in his tracks to take in Mireille's resplendent black gown.

"Truly," he said. "There is no rush. The moon has not yet turned. There is still time."

Real fear rested beneath his tone, and Mireille's heart pinched. That Thomas would have done anything so nearly an outburst revealed how dire he believed the situation was. Perhaps he thought her under some sort of thrall, like the spell that came over her in sleep. Closing the distance, she gripped his arms through his coat. "Thomas, please trust me."

His mouth sealed into a grim line. He had known the possibilities when they had come, that she might truly be bound to the prince, but Mireille hadn't realized just how deeply he had hoped to find information that might defeat the fae queen, to somehow free Mireille from her impossible situation.

"I do not need you to save me, Thomas. I will save myself, and we, fate willing, will save Norcliffe."

For a dizzying moment, the image of a different future than either would have ever planned swam before her, but she pressed it down. Mireille would uphold her part of the bargain, and if it worked, they would save Norcliffe. She and Thomas would return home. They would leave all of this— the fae prince and his magical court—behind. There would be no midnight walks in moonlit gardens, no sculpture that seemed to come alive, no Kin, no Noal, no dinners over well-worn books in a dimly lit study.

She would never again find Alder, eyes dark and jaw ticking, meeting her gaze across a long table, never again catch the stray twist to his lips that hinted he might own a true smile.

Thomas must have seen something in her expression that convinced him, because finally, he raised a hand to pat hers where it still gripped his arm. "I am here. All you need do is ask."

His words were not the comfort either of them may have wanted, because Mireille did need to ask something of him, and he wasn't going to like it one whit. Before they left, she leaned forward to whisper it into Thomas's ear.

CHAPTER 15

"We gave you what help we could," Noal said as he walked at Mireille's side, the halls empty of any other fae.

She managed a small smile as they approached the study. "I will repay you all the same courtesy."

The edge of his mouth tightened with a hint of concern as he reached for the door. Before it opened, he said, "I do hope you're as clever as you are confident, Highness."

"As do I," Mireille breathed. She gave the man a small curtsy, then strode into the study as if already a queen.

Alder stood behind his desk, dressed, unsurprisingly, in solid black, the embroidery on his coat a match to Mireille's gown. Only his crown broke the inky blackness, resting low on his head as he watched her with eyes like flecks of obsidian.

Noal darted a glance between the pair of them, and Mireille became aware they'd been staring at each other for a bit too long.

Noal cleared his throat and turned toward the prince. "Have you any further need of me?"

The prince's gaze had not strayed from Mireille. "Only to remind you of your duty to secure the perimeter."

Noal flinched. Mireille had to bite down the rebuke she wanted to snap at the prince. It had not been Noal's fault, and they both knew it. The prince had said he was certain the queen had been responsible, even though she could not break the laws of hospitality directly. It was clear that even far from her own court and bound by ancient tenets, she was a threat.

But the prince could not let on that he was not falling for her traps.

Alder stepped around the desk, offering Mireille his arm. She took it, lifting her chin to hide her apprehension. He must have noticed regardless, because he lightly gripped her wrist and shifted her arm to draw her more snuggly against him. The feeling that bloomed in her chest was not merely fear, but a sense of hope. Partnership. They both needed rid of the queen. They were in it together.

And afterward... Afterward she would be freed from her bargain. She would return home, and Alder could find whatever princess he wanted. If she felt a tremble of unease at the idea, she could not be blamed for it, or whatever dark and frenzied thoughts chased after.

Because, after all, the princess was about to lower herself to the role of *bait*.

THE HALL that Mireille had first encountered on her palace tour had transformed, its long row of arched windows draped with sheer curtains that dampened the midday sun. Long tables were bedecked with tiny sandwiches, tarts, cheeses, and platters mounded with fruit that looked plump and ripe enough to burst. Mireille's stomach tightened. She could not quite recall when she'd last eaten, but did not think she could steady herself enough to do it now.

Servers in crisp blue livery with polished buttons walked between the tables offering punch to those seated. It was a relief to find not half as many fae as had been present at the ball. Perhaps only certain members of the court had been invited. The fae present did not seem especially reluctant to attend, despite the previous night's attack.

Mireille was escorted toward a narrow table upon a raised dais. Nisha was already seated, her posture that of a cat considering play, her gown pale lavender with jeweled buttons up long cuffs that met billowing sleeves. A sudden sensation of being watched came over Mireille, despite that the entire gathering had their eyes on her, and she turned to find the queen swanning in through the main entrance, her gaze daggers. The collar of her crimson dress rose high in an artful swirl of red embroidery, her matching red lips in a contemptuous line.

Mireille could not wait to wipe the expression from her face. Alder had not explained precisely why the betrothal would be such a blow to the queen, aside from it ending her game, but Mireille suspected there was more to it, and that the *more* was tied to his curse. For her part, Mireille understood exactly why the queen would not want it to be her.

She hoped she'd been right to trust the prince. She hoped that while she had agreed to act as bait, she would not be left to become prey.

Mireille's chair was pulled out, and she sat stiffly, keeping her head high and her slippered feet flat on the floor. The crowd of fae were seated or standing near the line of windows, attention on the actions of their prince. A human dressed in fae garb was holding a position of honor at his side, in the presence of an enemy queen.

Nisha leaned close to murmur, "I did not believe you would truly manage it, Princess. Well done."

Alder twitched irritably, evidently having heard the remark. He lifted a glass and the room fell silent. It was a chilling reminder of the dinner at which he'd seemed to arrest time, but he had not used magic to still this room, only the power of his station. He said, "A soul's greatest desire is to find its match. One wishes, in their deepest depths, to marry not for duty or honor, but for that which is the incomparable prize,"—he looked at Mireille— "the bond that is love."

It took everything in Mireille's being to not react. She had expected a more politic announcement, not... sentiment. But she supposed they had been joined by a shared bond, the love for their people, their land, and their kingdoms. She raised her glass toward him.

"Two souls, bound together in a shared intent, equal in all and cherished above all else." His head inclined infinitesimally, then turned back toward the crowd. "So it is, with great pleasure, that I announce my engagement to Princess Mireille of Norcliffe."

He offered a gloved hand and she took it to stand. He had not said that he loved her, not truly. And she wasn't certain Alder couldn't lie. He had said *what is a lie but intent*. But if his intention had been to convince Maeve that he was serious, the words seemed to have done the trick. The fae queen's eyes were wide, her jaw agape, and the color had drained out of her cheeks.

Nisha was the first to break the silence, squawking out a sharp cheer that had the crowd joining in in surprise, even if scattered murmurs of confusion lingered. It was not clear if they understood that she was not a princess of Westrende and could not bring down the Rive, only that Nisha beamed at the pair. Nisha, who would take Alder's place if something were to happen to him.

Alder raised Mireille's hand to his lips, meeting her gaze as he laid a gentle kiss on her knuckles. She couldn't quite look away, and in the moment, on a dais in front of a crowd, her imaginings again went places they should not, places that could never become true.

It was a foolish thing to believe you might best your enemies when they had handed you the knife.

Nisha stood. "Let the celebrations begin!" She raised a glass, then glanced at it in disappointment. "Bring out something with a bit more kick!"

Servers leapt into motion and the chatter among the crowd became something that felt more genuinely of delight. Alder snaked an arm around Mireille's waist, drew her close, and lowered his lips to her ear. "You've done well, but we still must make her believe."

Feigning a chuckle at his words, Mireille slid her gaze toward where Maeve sat with a half-empty wine flute in hand. Her eyes were narrowed, scrutinizing the pair. Mireille quickly turned back to Alder. She had to stand on her toes, resting one palm on his chest to reach his ear. "I will do what must be done," she whispered.

"So accommodating," he rumbled with no small hint of irony. "Perhaps, at least, you could appear as if,"—he drew back to look at her, and his gaze darkened— "as if in the blush of new love."

Her smile was shaky. "Indeed, I have not blushed easily since I was a girl. Only when taken off guard."

A hum slipped out of him, then he leaned closer, voice low. "If I were to confess that I find you impossibly beautiful, that when you entered this room, head held high, in that dress..." his gaze trailed lower, then met hers once more. "You are every bit a queen, Mireille, and not a soul in this room would fault me for wanting—"

She pressed a single finger over his lips. "I fear, dear prince, that you are about to deliver insult with that line of supposed flattery."

His jaw flexed.

She let her fingertip trail slowly off his lips, then whispered. "If you'd like, you may try again. But I warn you, a princess does not blush easily."

Alder's gaze never left hers as he slid a hand over hers where it rested on his chest. Then he lowered his mouth to hers.

Mireille's heart thundered, all thoughts of pretense abandoning her. His lips were real, and warm, and drowning out every sense of the crowd around them. She was kissing the Prince of Rivenwilde, an unquestionably deadly fae in possession of ancient power and, fate help her, she liked it. Bergamot filled her senses, her fingers curled into the material of his jacket, and Mireille melted against him. He had managed to bring heat to her skin, that much was certain, but worse, he'd brought it to her chest, where her fool heart lived in an ocean of hope.

When he broke the kiss, drawing back with an unsteady emotion that may have been surprise, Mireille had no notion of what he might find in her own expression. An instant later though, he seemed to remember himself, and it was all erased by a charming smile. A smile meant, surely, for the fae queen alone.

They returned to their seats, and Mireille's flute was the first to be filled. A pungent liquor scent rose from the glass, and when Alder leaned toward her, his nearness sent an awareness through her she was not quite prepared to face.

"I don't recommend you drink that," he said against her ear.

Bait, she remembered. She was meant to drag the queen

from her perch. And with the lingering sensation of Alder's kiss still upon her lips and the terrible sensation of having softened toward the fae, she would need to keep her wits about her more than ever.

CHAPTER 16

The festivities wore on past nightfall, with Maeve's agitation seeming to increase by the hour. By the time Alder stood to escort Mireille to her chambers on the pretense of her needing rest—not entirely a fabrication as she was utterly exhausted from the day's nerves—Maeve was watching the pair with open hunger. She would most certainly take the bait.

Mireille took Alder's arm, avoiding Maeve's sharp gaze as they walked past. Beyond the enchanted doors that shut out the sounds of revelry, they walked in silence until they reached the entrance to Mireille's suite. "Do you think she'll—"

Alder held a finger to her lips, and it immediately recalled when she'd done the same to him, and the kiss that followed. She had to bite down a curse at her foolish heart, picking up pace in her chest. He did not care about her. He needed her only to trap the queen.

He said, "I vowed to protect you. You are safe."

She stared up at him, aware they were standing far closer

than was necessary. None of it was real; it was only a pretense, a show for the queen. "Of course."

His brow furrowed at her curt reply, but she stepped back, slipping into her room and closing the door behind her.

Despite asking Thomas to trust in her judgement, she hadn't been certain he would give way easily until she found the room empty. Suddenly, Alder's plan seemed like a terrible idea. She glanced at the closed door. *Safe*, the prince had said. As safe as she could be, under the circumstances. Midnight would come, and perhaps she would visit the tree. Perhaps she would once again know her father and their people were safe as well.

Or perhaps the queen would come to call instead.

Removing the formal gown, she wrapped herself not only in a nightshift, but a thick silk dressing gown, then crawled into bed. The land and its law and the prince's vow might protect her in the waking world, but the safety of dreams was not as faithful. Heaviness fell over her.

Mireille walked barefoot down a corridor she recognized, only it was not quite the same as it had been before. The walls seemed to breathe with the pulse of magic and the silver embroidery of her black gown shone unnaturally bright in the moonlight that streaked the stone floor. It was a dream, not the mindless midnight wandering she'd done under the queen's power. But Alder was nowhere in sight. And weren't they supposed to be laying a trap for the queen? She could not quite remember.

Her feet continued forward despite her concern, compelled to bring her to the familiar door at the end of the hallway. Unlike the other wanderings, Mireille was entirely aware of the fear gripping her heart, and yet, she pushed open the heavy door.

The hourglass that centered the room seemed brighter than before, and there, in the dream, Mireille understood it was a curse clock, counting down until the terms would end. Less sand rested at the top than when she'd last seen it, and as she watched, another grain fell. It glowed, ethereal in the shadowed room, like a shell dropped through water, sunlight catching on its nacre. The fall of sand had sped. The prince was running out of time.

"Perhaps I *should* have made you my spy."

The queen's voice was playful, but it turned Mireille's blood to ice.

Maeve stepped from the shadows, still wearing the crimson gown. Foxglove and lilac clung to the scent of her magic, as if trying to hide the power that pricked Mireille's skin. Maeve said, "You already know this room, else you would not have found the way." Her gaze turned speculative. "But Alder would not have shown it to you."

"You cursed him." Mireille's voice revealed no hint of tremor, though her body felt sick with fear. It was true, she could feel it. The queen's magic was everywhere, but it centered on the clock.

Maeve tilted her head, one corner of her wide mouth tipping up. "No." Then she leaned forward. "Let me tell you a story, Princess, like they do in Westrende. Once upon a time, a handsome prince of the fae was trapped in a curse he did not create. The land was broken, his father was dead, and the prince was desperate. Tragic, really. Suffering all around. You know the way. But one day, a beautiful queen appeared with an offer. And that poor prince, well he had nothing left to lose, so he gambled it all. Twice the cost of the curse for a slim nothing chance to break it."

The queen straightened. "You humans love to believe that the noble-born are noble of character, but the fae never do. You see, pet, he was not cursed by me. He accepted my bargain of his own free will."

Her gaze traveled over Mireille. "For a time, he held out

hope that he would beat me, but he has obviously grown desperate with this—" she waved her hand disdainfully in Mireille's direction, "charade."

Mireille swallowed hard, at both the explanation and the accusation. She knew well enough why the queen had come for her. It was not simply to win Norcliffe. "There is no charade. We will wed, and he will win."

"Oh truly? You expect me to believe that he has fallen in love with you, and you him?" She snorted. "Absurd. You come all the way from Norcliffe, show up on his steps like a lost pup, innocent and meek, and he's supposed to fall for your ruse?" Her voice dipped dangerously. "He will never love you."

Mireille's palms broke into sweat and she did not know if the sensation was real or conjured by the queen. She only knew that both Alder and the queen had mentioned love, as if it were a term of their bargain.

Two bindings, a curse and a bargain. Two requirements to break them.

Maeve grinned at Mireille's shifting expression. "I see he has not told you the full truth. And yet, you trusted him, fool that you are. You would not be the first to fall for it, I assure you. The prince does have a certain," she rolled her hand again in that dismissive gesture, "*charm*, but I had thought you cleverer than that. Cleverer than the others." She edged closer, and Mireille had to fight her every instinct in order to remain still. It was only a dream. Maeve wasn't controlling her. She could not be harmed, not there.

Maeve whispered, "But I can offer you a way out."

Mireille gritted her teeth. "I do not wish to escape. I have made my choice."

"Princess, there *is* no choice." Maeve lifted her hands as she approached the curse clock. "Your wish is to save your kingdom, and I am the only one who can grant it."

Mireille's hands curled into fists. "You are the very danger it faces."

Maeve shot her a self-satisfied grin. "Precisely. And so, if you would like to save your kingdom, you will do exactly as I say." She stroked the hourglass, expression gone dark. "You will let Alder believe you are his accomplice until the last moment, but you will keep your distance, treat him as coldly as a viper, for that is what he is to you. You will tell not a soul of your plans. And when time is nearly up, when he believes he has won and outwitted us both, you will forsake him. When the moon is high, all of Rivenwilde gathered round, triumph will finally be mine."

When it was too late for Alder to find someone new. But Mireille understood there was no one else. Only she was left as a threat to the queen.

And the prince's time would be out. The price of breaking Mireille's bargain with the prince was her cooperation. If she turned against him, chose her kingdom over defeating the queen, it would be to spend eternity in Rivenwilde. Not as Alder's wife, but his prisoner. But the safety of Norcliffe would rely solely on the promises of a treacherous queen.

Maeve lifted a finely arched brow. "I see that you are concerned. If your fear is in regard to your bargain to marry the prince, do not fret. Once Rivenwilde is mine, I can set you free. You would not remain a prisoner of the prince for long. And I will never bother Norcliffe again. You would have my word."

Mireille's heart pounded in her ears. Surely, the queen meant that she would merely be *her* prisoner instead. And if she refused, well Maeve had proven what she wanted for Mireille. It was of no consequence how: a dagger, a fall, at the hands of her guard. Alder had wanted the queen near to win the protection provided by the laws of hospitality, and perhaps that was all that was preventing Maeve from ending Mireille right then.

With Alder's plan, Mireille was walking a dangerous line, balanced on the edge of a blade. Now the blade itself offered a promise. She stood tall. "I will make my choice on the altar."

"And what choice will that be? The false promises of a broken prince, doomed to lose all, or the vow of a clever queen who only grows in power?" Her magic swelled through the room. "It is not often I make such a generous offer to one such as you. I assure you, it will be the last."

"I would be a fool not to take it."

Maeve's grin was full of teeth. "I see we understand each other."

CHAPTER 17

The next morning, Mireille was dead on her feet. Alder had not come for her in dreams. He had expected Mireille would rise from her bed under Maeve's control. He would have been waiting nearby to save her, silently listening at the door, or watching her sleep from the shadows. They had bet on the queen breaking the rules of hospitality while a guest under his roof. Without Mireille having left the bed, he would have assumed the queen had not visited her at all.

But Maeve had broken no rules. Mireille had not been harmed. She had opened the door to the room that held the queen of her own free will. They had not trapped the queen. So, Mireille would make a choice—give in to Maeve's demands, or trust that Alder would defeat her.

The prince's plan still had merit. It had made the queen desperate enough to vow to give up Norcliffe. Mireille might never know the details of her bargain with the prince. It was the reason, after all, that they could not be spoken. If one could simply ask for help, cursebreaking would be far less complicated.

Would that Mireille's own problems might be managed so easily, when the queen had twisted even Norcliffe's most loyal against the kingdom itself. The only person who might have a chance to help was Alder.

A brief knock sounded at the door before Thomas let himself in. He looked as bad as Mireille felt, his blue coat wrinkled and his golden hair mussed. "Still alive, I see." The playfulness she knew he intended fell a bit flat. Thomas was tired, and not just from lack of sleep.

"Have faith, Thomas."

He raised a brow. "You look as if you've tussled a bear."

She ran a hand over her hair, and it snagged on the cuff of her gown. "I am perfectly well. I have no other choice; there's a long day of wedding planning ahead of us."

Thomas stepped closer, lowering his voice. "Rei, talk to me. Let me help."

She turned toward the mirror, making a show of sorting her hair.

To her back, Thomas said, "The queen herself is in this very palace, and you are acting as if it's of little consequence. He betrayed you, before the month was even up."

She dropped her arms. "Coming apart at the seams would do no good. Once the ceremony is over, I can quail about however I like." One way or the other, it would be decided.

He reached up to flick a fingernail against a fresh orange blossom in the tabletop vase. "And our kingdom will be left without its heir."

She flinched, she couldn't help it. In the mirror, she met his gaze. "You know me, Thomas. Please, just this once, I need you to not ask questions."

"You brought me here as your advisor. My entire purpose is to ask questions."

Mireille crossed the distance to face him. "For now, I only need you to be my friend."

He studied her for a long, tense moment. Just when she thought he might turn his back on her, he sighed. "I will always be your friend. Even if it means planning a wedding to a pompous, conniving fae."

She chuckled, feeling able to truly breathe for the first time in days. "He is rather pompous, is he not?"

THE DAYS PASSED QUICKLY, planning for a wedding that, if either the queen or Alder had their wish, would not truly be, and the turning of the moon loomed ever closer. Mireille had Alder's vow that if she participated in his scheme, she would fulfill the price of breaking their bargain and he would set her free. But she would only truly be free if he succeeded in vanquishing the queen, and of that she had no guarantee. Maeve's magic had not visited Mireille again, and without the threat of the queen, Alder had not come to her in dreams.

With any luck neither would have to see the queen until the wedding. The wedding at which Mireille was meant to betray the prince.

A dark part of Mireille wanted to accept the queen's offer, to grasp onto the slender chance that she might truly leave Norcliffe alone. Outside of the bargain, she owed no allegiance to Alder. But sometimes, when midnight brewed and memories rose, the remembered sands of the hourglass landed like stones in her heart. She did not know what losing his bargain to the queen would cost Alder, or the kingdom of Rivenwilde. Saving her own people was one thing, allowing evil to prey upon others was something else entirely.

The tip of her finger welled with blood and she cursed,

pressing it into her mouth. She'd been picking at tattered threads from an embroidery piece, hoping it would clear her mind. It hadn't worked. Now she was agitated *and* bleeding.

When a knock sounded at her door, she tossed the tangled mess aside and hurried to answer. Kin swept into the room wearing a deep blue day dress and a broad grin. Mireille stared at the gown she displayed, emotions fighting inside her chest. Kin nodded, shifting the gown for better view, and Mireille walked slowly closer, approaching the creation as if it were a predator.

It was the dream gown. Every piece of lace, the flowing train, all of it exactly as her mind had conjured. "How?" she breathed.

Kin's brow furrowed, but Mireille could not explain that she had dreamed the dress—a wedding gown, to her horror—and suddenly it was real and true before her.

Mireille ran a fingertip carefully over the material. It was exactly her taste, the lace soft as flower petals, and the cut like something from an earlier century. Romantic, like a maiden in the paintings she'd adored as a girl, the women from tales who escaped a medieval keep to run away with the hero of their dreams. Fates, was that where she had taken inspiration? Mireille would have never admitted to longing for such a garment in the waking world, not to anyone. And yet, there it was.

He had it made for you, Kin signed. *The seamstress said he was very specific.*

Had she a shell, Mireille might have crawled into it. But her finger continued to trace the soft lace. *It's beautiful,* she signed, the motions coming more smoothly given her practice with Kin. *Thank you for bringing it.*

Kin curtseyed, but there was something hesitant in her expression.

What is it? Mireille signed.

The woman chewed her lip, but only shook her head. She gestured for Mireille to try it on.

Well, look at that, Mireille thought at her reflection. *He* can *make you blush*. It did not bode well for the coming ceremony, the closest she might get to a marriage with the prince.

Whatever choice she made, whatever bargain she placed her fate in, neither involved completing the ceremony. If what she suspected was true, Alder would not be merely giving up on his kingdom if he married her, but far more. Because it must be someone he loved, someone who loved him in return. Not Mireille.

Not that it mattered. She was a princess of Norcliffe. She would always choose what was best for her kingdom. It just... it didn't make sense that he would go to the trouble of designing the dress. Maeve had never seen it. No one but Mireille and Alder would ever know.

She could ask him. He may not be able to tell her details of his curse, but he could tell her that.

But gowns did not matter. They hoped to trap for the queen before the ceremony. All that mattered was that. Mireille had come to Rivenwilde to find a way to save her kingdom, and every step they took was closer to her last chance.

She stood numbly as Kin laced the bodice. In stockinged feet, she moved closer to the tall mirror, taking it in. He had remembered every detail, after only seeing it only once. Mireille remembered too. It was how she knew the dress was perfect. Kin beamed in the reflection behind her, and Mireille forced a smile in return. Dinner with Alder was only hours away, as they had been doing their best to keep up appearances. If she had begun to look forward to their quiet evenings in his study, reading in companionable silence or laughing over something Noal had said, if she had found herself anxious to return to the dreams, it was only that time was so close. That so much was on the line.

It could be nothing more.

CHAPTER 18

That evening, Mireille strolled through the palace in search of a quiet place to sit, open to the night air. Wandering in the direction she believed to be where she'd seen the butterflies before, she came across a towering archway carved with foxes and rabbits chasing through the marble foliage. She passed beneath the archway, staring up at a scene with squirrels scampering over an apple tree, branches twining in shapes reminiscent of ancient knots and leaves. Head tilted back, spinning slowly in place to take it all in, Mireille caught the scent of wisteria blossoms.

Focus snapping toward the garden beyond, she tracked the scent, on the hunt herself, passing through vine-covered trellises and over a small stone bridge. Tall statues rose from the garden, maidens like the ones inside the palace. All seemed to point her toward the center of the courtyard, where stood the wisteria tree of her dreams.

Strange emotions rolled through her as she stared on, each as unsettling as the last. The tree had been real, and inside her dreams. Alder had taken her to the heart of Rivenwilde. She moved closer, taking in the scene in the light of a lowering sun. The boughs hung heavy, brushing her shoulders as she walked beneath, her palm itching to touch the bark. It might be devastating if it were only a tree, if the magic had been only a dream, but she had no choice but to try.

When her hand brushed the bark, its warmth spread through her, and with it, emotions even sharper than she'd felt during her dreams. Norcliffe was there, safe and stable, and her father, too. But while sensing him offered the comfort that he was well, she could feel that he worried for Mireille. He worried for her, and for Thomas, for his kingdom, and for so much more.

He prayed they'd done right to send her away. His wished Mireille's mother was still alive.

"Oh, Papa," she whispered, and it was as if, somehow, he heard her speak. A spark of joy snapped through the tree, feeling of relief and confusion and the fear that came with the unfamiliar. "Papa," she said again. "It's me. I'm in the fae lands and I am safe. I wish you could see it. I wish I could see you. But I will one day, and all will be well." Her fingers curled against the bark, and her chest tightened with the desire to weep. "I miss you, Papa. And I love you. Please do not worry over me."

The tree seemed to sigh, then the warmth slipped away, and all that remained beneath Mireille's palm was the smooth bark of a tree she was fairly certain was a type used to concoct poisons. She drew her hand free, stepping back with a chest so tight she felt as if she could not get enough air. Uncertain she would be able to find it again, she tore the ribbons from her gown and tied them along the path until she reached the palace walls.

But the archway she'd entered before was gone. All that stood in its place was a pair of plain tall columns. The ribbons fell from her hands.

When she turned again, the garden was gone, and only an empty lawn stretched before her.

NOAL ARRIVED PRECISELY on time to escort Mireille to Alder's study. There was no talk of the prince being too busy, or of her taking her meal in her rooms. It had become routine. Until Nisha stormed out of the study door, nearly barreling into them.

She was dressed like springtime, pale pink satin with trailing violet ribbons and what might have been actual, living flowers attached at the hem. Her focus narrowed on Mireille and Noal. "You, the pair of you. Talk sense into him. The proper rites must be observed." Her tone dipped. "I will not be robbed of this." She marched off, leaving Mireille and Noal to stare after.

Noal said, "I'll just... Fetch your meals, shall I?" then turned and walked the other direction.

"Traitor," Mireille hissed at his back.

Straightening her spine, she strode into the study.

Alder stood behind his desk, pinching the bridge of his nose, face downcast. He lifted his gaze upon her entry, then crossed the room to shut the door, sealing them alone inside. "My sister."

She turned to him. "Your sister."

He stepped closer, letting out a tired breath as his dark eyes met hers. "My sister is insisting on ceremonial rites. Traditionally, three nights before a Riven Court marriage ceremony, the bride is taken to a sacred pool where ancient fae rites are performed."

"Oh." Her hand wanted to clutch at the fabric of her

dress, but she forced it to still. "I'm not certain I like the sound of that." Pools were excellent places to drown.

"The rite must be completed by another female," Alder continued. "Nisha has decided it will be her. She has vowed your protection, and she will do as she's vowed. She would not misstep when it would cost her title."

"You make it sound as if it's already decided."

His expression was pained. "It is your choice. But, as it's sacred tradition among all of court, it would look especially suspicious for the bride of a prince to not participate."

Mireille crossed her arms over her waist, feeling suddenly vulnerable. She had agreed to cooperate with Alder's plan. Suspicion would not do. But there was still one issue. "Three nights before the ceremony is—"

"Tonight," Alder finished.

A sacred rite at some fae pool with only Nisha to keep her safe. The queen had ceased her attempts at stealing into Mireille's sleep, and Nisha would not be bent by the fae magic the way it came over Thomas. But they would be outside the protections of the palace. "Is there another reason this ritual so important to Nisha?"

Mireille must have said something wrong, because he straightened. "She may be scheming and duplicitous, but she is still my sister. And she will regard you as a sister the moment we are wed."

The words hung heavy between them. It did not matter that there would be no marriage, because Nisha did not know Alder's plan. It mattered that she believed, the same as the queen. Mireille nodded. "And what of protections once I leave the palace?"

Alder's posture eased, hinting that the ritual was not important only to his sister, but to him as well. "Nisha has given her vow. It is a bond that can be trusted nearly as much as my own." Chin dipping, he gave her an especially dark look. "But I will be near, nonetheless."

"It sounded as if you were not invited."

"I am, as of yet, still the prince of Rivenwilde. I may go where I choose."

She didn't like that it felt as if Nisha would not be aware of his proximity, or that she would be forced to rely so thoroughly on trust, or that she did not seem to have a choice in the matter. There was a great deal not to like about the entire ordeal. "Very well," she said. "The matter is decided."

He seemed at once relieved and on edge. On impulse, Mireille touched his arm. Her mouth opened to ask him why he'd ever agreed to bargain with the queen in the first place. She wanted to ask if the terms had been twisted, if he had thought to marry a princess of Westrende, to fall in love. She wanted to ask about the curse clock, and why it seemed he no longer believed he might fulfill the queen's price.

But she could not, for Mireille understood both that the queen was listening, and that she, and her father, and everyone she loved had nearly given up on defeating the queen, too. There was no room for notions of romance. Their only hope was the same sort of trickery the queen used against them. Their only hope was to work together to end her reign.

Hand still on his arm, she said, "Just tell me what I need to do."

His gaze was searching, but she did not reveal more. She would give Alder's plan a chance, and if it seemed it would fail, she would be forced to betray him, to choose the offer presented by the enemy queen.

Princesses did not have the luxury of following their hearts. And neither did fae princes. They had both proven as much already.

NISHA'S MOOD was radiant as she guided Mireille through a dark and eerie wood. They both wore flowing white gowns, as did the flock of fae courtiers trailing after them.

Thomas had thought Mireille mad for agreeing to any of it, and she could not argue that. But it had been Noal who convinced Thomas of Mireille's safety. A fae vow meant more than either had understood. It was not merely the binds of a reputation or the value of a person's word, it had to do with the very magic they possessed. Evidently, fae magic was not one-sided. It could punish those who broke the rules.

A low growl sounded from the spiky bushes ahead, but none of the fae women paid it mind. Mireille suspected, as Nisha tugged her hand, urging her to keep up in the thick growth, that nothing in the forest was as feral as the fae princess she'd agreed to follow.

Nisha's sigh sounded of anticipation. "My mother would have loved this. She never had a chance to perform the rite, and she was particularly fond of Alder."

"Is she residing at the Storm Court?" Mireille asked weakly, barely navigating the roots jutting up through the path.

Nisha lifted her free hand to her chest. "I'm touched you remembered. But no, she passed on long ago. Alder and I only share a father. We are glad at least that he's long gone." She glanced sidelong at Mireille, not having to say aloud that she was surprised he'd not mentioned their family history.

The path widened, leading to a large mere, its surface glimmering in the moonlight. Nisha came to a stop, as if taking in the scene, a wide smile changing her face. She looked younger somehow, full of magic and mischief. It was not an entirely comforting idea.

The rest of the group hurried around them, lighting torches and candles, and arranging a stunning array of food on cloth spread over the ground. In all her wildest imaginings, Mireille would never have guessed that her bargain would lead there, a moonlit picnic in a deadly forest.

And then there was the pool, magical waters in which she would be submerged, a symbol of her acceptance of the land and its power as her life merged with its prince. She resisted the urge to look for Alder, who had promised he would be near, watching on should any of it go sideways.

Nisha squeezed the hand she'd been holding, then released it. "I'll fetch us something to drink."

When she returned with two long-stemmed glasses, the rest of the preparations seemed nearly done. Mireille took a sip of the sharp, citrusy punch then drew a breath of crisp night air. A fire had been built near the edge of the mere, a relief, given that she was meant to step into water, but she was beginning to doubt her bravery.

She had vowed to do anything for her kingdom. Surely walking into an ominous midnight pool would be the least of it. And as vexing as Nisha could be, the prince clearly cared about her and about the ritual. It must have been important, and in the end, they plainly expected her to remain safe.

Nisha led Mireille to one of the cloths bedecked with silver tureens of roast venison, bright steamed vegetables, and sourdough bread. It smelled as wonderful as any feast she'd ever attended, though that may have been owing to the arduous trek. Settling onto the ground, wine in one hand and plate in the other, Mireille finally felt the return of warmth.

"Now," Nisha said. "Tell us exactly how you and my brother came to fall in love."

Mireille nearly choked. The others watched with interest.

"Go on," Nisha pressed. "Declare your intentions to us and to the moon. Your words will not leave this circle."

To be sure, the circle was not Mireille's chief concern, it was Alder, possibly listening nearby from the shadows. Clearing her throat, she set aside her plate.

Nisha frowned. "You do love him, do you not? At the announcement, he implied it was a love match."

Mireille had watched fae slide a lie cleverly around the truth, certainly by now she could do it too. She forced a shaky laugh. "Well, I am marrying him and giving up my kingdom, after all. It would be absurd not to love him, all things considered."

Nisha's posture eased, but her clear expectation did not.

"I suppose my feelings for him changed from the first night we danced. We were alone in a moonlit ballroom, soft music coming in through the windows..." She sighed at the memory, because it seemed so long ago, and was not unaware that her audience had taken it as wistful longing. "It was just the two of us, no thought of responsibility, only the melody and the steps. It's such a rare thing as the head of a kingdom. As a girl, I cherished such moments when my father gave them to me." Lips pursed, she tried to recall what else she might share. "And then later, again when we found ourselves alone, walking through such beautiful gardens, speaking low of the things that matter most to us. You can tell a lot about a person when there are no crowds, no courtiers to impress."

The fae women leaned in, hanging on her every word, and Mireille struggled to find more that was safe to share. At the very least, she could toy with the man at bit, should he be listening. She said, "At the outset, he seemed so gruff, but it turns out he was never surly at all. He's quite gentle under all that starch and frippery. Like a sugarplum." That drew a chuckle from the group, but they did not seem sated. "Of course, he has a great many duties, and would never succumb to idle pleasures, but he's, well he can be generous and giving. So entirely thoughtful that he—"

Mireille's words cut off, her face gone hot. She'd nearly detailed the dream gown for an audience. Perhaps she'd had too much punch. The women seemed too close, but so did the moon. Or, perhaps it was the influence of fae magic, because she had surely not just been going on about the prince in front of both him and a crowd. She glanced at the prince's sister.

Nisha's grin was wicked, and more than a little satisfied. She stood, offering Mireille her hand. "Come. It's time."

AT THE WATER'S EDGE, they removed their boots. Nisha stood beside Mireille, and barefoot, they walked together toward the pool, the rest of the fae watching from the bank.

The water was so cold Mireille gasped. She spared a moment to think of Thomas, warm by the fire in his chambers but probably worried sick. She hoped they'd been right to tell him she was safe, and she hoped their time away had given him a chance to complete the favor she'd asked of him.

Water closed around her legs, filling her with the sensation of movement. If it was magic, it was a gentle sort, like the wisteria tree. It seemed to promise it would not harm her, even if it smelled a bit of bad cabbage.

And she had just gone and blindly trusted it, the way she had trusted everything Alder said.

The crash of breaking glass was followed by female shouts and screams. Nisha spun, grabbing hold of Mireille's wrist. A monstrous shadow with strange glimmering eyes flung one of the fae ladies aside, then another as the woman rushed it with a violent cry.

It was a thing of nightmares, nothing like the creature that had attacked Mireille on her first night. It stood taller than any man, its claws formed entirely of darkness. The thing's eyes never came off Mireille. There was no question it was there for her as it released a hungry growl and lunged toward the pool.

Nisha shoved Mireille behind her, then leapt toward the creature, transforming mid-air not into a slender mink, but a sleek and massive beast, as large as a lion and jaws spread wide. The shadow creature shrieked. Nisha's cat-like claws sunk into its chest, and they both splashed down into the water.

The force of their impact shoved Mireille back and into a deeper pool. She tried to kick out but could no longer reach the earth beneath. Unseen hands pressed her suddenly down, beneath the surface and into complete darkness. Body spinning, she couldn't find which way was up. She inhaled a lungful of earthy water. She'd always been a strong swimmer, but her limbs floated uselessly, the weight pressing around her somehow far more than any sea.

A hand closed around her wrist.

She was jerked to the surface, gasping and choking the instant they broke through. She felt Alder behind her, one arm wrapped around her waist as she heaved out water.

When the heaving subsided, he brought her to the water's edge. Throat burning, eyes blurry, Mireille searched out the creature that had attacked. It was nowhere on the bank. Nisha, in her human form and dripping with both water and something thick and dark, scowled at Alder. "I had it under control."

Mireille glanced back at the water, and saw, finally, the

shadow creature unmoving, its skin smooth and onyx, the magic that had surrounded it gone.

"She nearly drowned." Alder's voice was cold, the rumble of it flush against Mireille's back, his arms still around her.

"I was handling it," Nisha repeated.

"We will argue at the palace."

Nisha appeared to want to argue right then and there, but with one look at Mireille, hanging wet and limp in Alder's grip, she nodded sharply instead.

CHAPTER 19

Mireille's stomach turned as the scenery shifted around them, then they were in Alder's study. He braced her while she tried to regain equilibrium, but there was no use. Drenched and with her lungs burning, she slumped against him. He lifted her effortlessly, carrying her toward a cushioned chair in the corner. After settling her gently upon it, he knelt at her feet, his dark eyes more earnest than she had ever seen. His jacket and crown were absent, his shirt soaked through. "Are you injured?"

She shook her head. "There was something in the water, but it only pressed me down." She pushed a strand of wet hair away from her face with a trembling hand.

His own hand lifted, as if to help, then stopped short. "You have my sincerest apologies that she was able to get that far. The queen was securely inside the palace, but her influence has clearly reached further than any of us knew." He stood. "This proves she believes our ruse, if nothing else. She is terrified we may go through with the ceremony, and that means she will try again."

Mireille's throat was raw. She felt as if she'd heaved up a

great deal more water than she had swallowed. "How many times does she have to attempt to kill me before we catch her?"

His gaze shot to hers. "The attempt must be hers, and then, only once. But she has bought her way to you, likely with bargains or threats. There will be no proving that she sent that creature tonight."

"Then how can you be certain that it was her? Surely there are more than a few from your own court who would see me dead."

His shoulder flexed beneath the damp shirt, and he jerked loose his cravat. "Because if it was a member of my court, I would have sensed it sooner. There was no warning before the creature attacked. He may have appeared to you the same as the shadow creatures that reside on our lands, but those loyal to the queen are a species entirely aside."

Mireille slumped into the cushions, aware that she was likely ruining a lovely piece of furniture, but unable to summon the energy to move. She'd made a mistake. She should have taken the queen's offer. "We didn't complete the rite."

He rolled a shoulder. "Nisha had her moment. She won't push again, especially after what happened. It's not as if—" He shook his head and Mireille had the sense he could not say what he'd wanted, that it did not matter whether the ceremony was complete, because she would never truly be his wife. He finished, "If the land accepts you, it will tell you itself. It will show you in its own way."

She picked a rogue leaf off the skirt of her gown, trying very hard not to think about the fact that the land had shown her its heart, the wisteria tree. "You were watching the entire time?"

"You played your part well."

Played her part. Because she had been acting, because none of it was real. She did not meet his gaze.

"You're shivering." Alder lightly touched her cheek. "How careless of me." Flames burst to life in the fireplace, licking across fresh logs as if they had been burning all night.

Sometimes, Mireille could almost forget he possessed bottomless magic, that he was just as fae as the queen. As if pulling her from that pool and transporting her to his study in the space of a breath wasn't reminder enough.

"I will take you to your chambers and have Kin draw a bath."

Mireille leaned closer to the hearth, her shivering nearly subsided. "I would like to stay for a bit, if you do not mind." At his pinched brow, she explained, "Thomas will be waiting in my chambers. I'd rather not let him see how wrongly tonight has gone."

"Ah. In that case..." A thick woven blanket appeared in his hand, another reminder of his magic, then he stepped forward, lightly draping it over her.

She drew the blanket closer. "Thank you for saving me."

"You were there at my request. I will not forget it."

"If it is a favor I'm owed, I fear I must ask it sooner rather than later." She bit her lip at the concern in his expression. "Show me your sculpture. I want to see the room where you work."

He ran a hand over his middle. "I was hoping you would not remember that."

"Highness, I have thought of little else."

He smiled softly at the comment, and it was maybe the most genuine one she'd seen. "Very well," he said finally. "Whenever you ask it of me."

"Now."

He frowned. "You are weak and wet and—"

"More of your flattery? Do stop, I've had all I can take. A

woman might swoon at any moment with such adulation." She stood, wrapping the blanket tightly around her, aware that the hem of her gown was still far too wet to drag over palace carpets. But at that moment, Mireille wanted nothing more than to discover what the prince of Rivenwilde would choose to immortalize with chisel and stone.

MIREILLE WAS SURPRISED to find herself transported to Alder's chamber. Had she known, she might have given the entire notion a second thought. As it was, she made a concerted effort not to stare at the spot by the writing desk where she'd picked up the paper knife weeks before. She glanced through the space, mostly unchanged from her last visit, but there were no sculptures to be found.

Shaking his head, he crossed in front of her to press his palm to the wood paneling. A portion swung open, and the prince gestured for Mireille to enter. As she did, candles lit one by one, their light flickering along the walls of another, larger chamber.

The space was scattered with countless workbenches, and bins holding rods, boards, and tools. It smelled of clay and oils, and of the dust that clung to every surface. She moved slowly forward, past blocks of stone, tables scattered with sketches, and the half-formed lines carved into pillars of marble and bronze. She could not be made to stop and consider them all, her gaze intent on a cluster of smaller works near the far wall. When she reached the wall, she gazed up, awestricken.

It was not many pieces, but one massive composition, flowers and creatures wound as intricately into the design as she'd seen in the archway that had led her to the wisteria tree, so lifelike she felt as though she might reach out to find petals and fur soft instead of stone.

Hand pressed to her chest, Mireille could only imagine Alder alone in the large open room, recreating every flower and form that touched the land, biding his time until the curse was broken. Trapped. Stripped of his full power. Beholden to the queen.

She nearly jumped when he spoke close behind her.

"It was unfair of me to goad you into playing for me, when it was obviously so painful."

She stiffened. His thoughts had evidently run perilously close to hers. She said, "I did so willingly."

"Still, I should have repaid you this favor then."

Stepping toward a large, canvas-covered piece, she said, "You have now." She could almost feel his discomfort when she neared it.

He said, "There are some interesting studies over here, you need not trouble with that older work."

Mireille reached forward to drag the canvas aside. Orange blossoms. So real she could smell their gentle scent. The white petals were rimmed with the finest grooves, their stamens molded in bronze. She glanced over her shoulder at Alder. She had yet to uncover the significance of the blossoms, and it was clear this piece had a significance of its own.

He moved close to her side. "They did not always exist here. My mother planted them when she arrived. They were her favorite, a reminder of her home, and she spent a great deal of time guiding them into what they are today. The avenue is a sacred place. Forbidden to those who walk the grounds." His gaze met hers. "I'm afraid I was showing off a bit when I allowed you and Thomas to approach the palace through that lane."

There was true sadness behind his words. It was not the

secret she had expected, but she understood it well. "My mother taught me the piano. When she grew weak, I played for her, every day until she was gone. I had not played again until—"

"Until I asked you to."

"You did not ask. I volunteered."

"Regardless, I cannot regret hearing you play. It was... I feel honored to have experienced it." His gaze was steady, even as color rose to her cheeks. "You miss her."

"Every day." Mireille's words were soft, barely a whisper.

"Tell me about her. Did she cherish growing up in Norcliffe as dearly as you?"

Candlelight glinted in his dark hair, still damp from the pond. The answer danced on the tip of her tongue, eager to share in the stories of her mother, stories she had rarely been able to reveal, but there were things she must keep to herself. Things that could be used against her. Things that might slam shut the narrow door that they'd opened. "Speaking of her is painful." The words were not exactly a lie, she had truly wanted to tell him, but that was a danger in itself.

"Of course. Forgive me." Expression suddenly guarded, Alder offered his arm. It was as if he had forgotten, as if he had been there only for her. And it was over once more. "I should escort you to your chamber. Surely Thomas is asleep by now."

He wouldn't be, but Mireille took the prince's arm anyway, casting one last longing glance at the sculpture as he led her from the room. The orange blossoms weren't some ancient magic, nor did they bear hidden symbolism. They simply revealed what Alder cherished, and the memories that kept him company in the long hours of the night.

CHAPTER 20

The following evening's dinner conversations with Alder had been noticeably stilted. Mireille had the sense the sands of his curse clock would run out as they stood before an altar beneath the moon—the fae were a theatrical sort—which meant that time was nearly up for both of them, as well as for their kingdoms. And if the queen obtained so much more power, she would be impossible to stop.

Maeve's offered bargain had clearly only been a precaution in the event that her assassination attempts failed. The queen must have believed Mireille and Alder could fall in love. If she had not, she would have nothing to fear. How strange that love was the thing a monster feared most.

Alder, for his part, had ordered Mireille watched almost *too* closely. Her first moment of peace came when Thomas had gone to the kitchens to fetch a snack. Alone in her chambers, she leaned back into the settee. But she'd no more than let out a sigh before the door opened to Noal, pushing a small, wheeled cart bedecked with cake.

Mireille frowned. "I thought we'd decided on the ceremony menu already."

Noal wheeled the cart to her, then took a step back. "Apparently the others have been deemed out of fashion. Princess Nisha awaits your opinion on this new selection."

She picked up a fork, examining the assortment. Strange little leaves and flowers adorned one, sugar sculptures of varying subjects topped the others. Perhaps she should have requested orange blossoms.

"There is a saying about throwing rocks at feeding lions," Noal said. When Mireille glanced up at him, he added, "Don't. That's the saying. Don't throw rocks at feeding lions."

"Lest you get eaten yourself?"

"Just that." He cleared his throat. "I suspect such a game is afoot, and I would be remiss to not say it seems a great folly, what the pair of you are about." He crossed his hands at the wrists, and for the first time, it came across less as a habitual gesture and one that felt as if he were performing a duty. "Mayhap, laying down arms would bring you far greater strength."

Noal was no fool. The man watched everything. She lifted a bite of cake to her lips, refusing to acknowledge the bit about her and Alder surrendering to each other. "I see no lion, only a spider, tangling her web tighter and tighter. And the only good way to be rid of spiders is to set their webs aflame."

"As long as the entire house doesn't burn down in the process."

"Noted," Mireille said.

"Shall I tell Nisha that you have made your choice?" He gestured toward the tray, though she had only tasted a sliver of one. It did not taste well, but they would all taste of ash in her mouth, given the circumstances. "Raspberry, I think." At least it looked pretty.

She cleared her throat against a tickle and reached for a glass. Her tongue felt a bit thick, and she coughed. By the time she lifted the glass to her lips, her airway had constricted.

Noal leaned forward, his eyes gone wide, posture stiff. Mireille stood, the glass fell from her hands, and with not a single word, she collapsed. He caught her just before she hit the ground. Fingers clawed into the material of his vest, she struggled to breathe, and her gaze met his. *Poison.* She'd been poisoned.

That was when she remembered. Nisha had not even been in the kitchens—she'd said he was going to the forest to collect some rare... *something* she'd meant to use in the decorations. Mireille let go of Noal, scrambled backwards, and knocked into the cart, porcelain shattering around her and tea pooling around her limp arms as blackness overtook her.

MIREILLE STARED up at a strange dark ceiling. She blinked, too exhausted to lift her hands and rub her bleary eyes. It was not her bed, not her chamber. Dragging every ounce of her will to shove down the emerald coverlet, she tried to sit up.

"You should not attempt to move." Alder's voice was thick. His shadowed form seemed to block out the rest of the room. A memory swam to the surface, and Mireille was unsure if it was real or a dream, Alders voice, *I shouldn't have let you out of my sight. Not even for a moment.*

"The cakes..." Her throat was raw. Her mouth tasted of medicinal herbs.

He stepped closer. "The queen has grown in power. Noal has been questioned extensively and, it seems, she was somehow able to influence him. The palace was swept, the staff interrogated, no stone left unturned." His jaw flexed. "She has more spies among us than I ever could have imagined. They are inside the palace. Our *home*."

Just as she had done in Norcliffe. Except that Noal had not been asleep. Mireille should have told Alder about the queen calling her to the room with the hourglass, when her magic had felt different and she had not taken full control. She fumbled to grab hold of his wrist; her fingers felt puffy and clumsy. "I am still here. She has failed. Tomorrow night is the ceremony."

He shook his head. "It was only because you tasted so little, else we would not have saved you." He let out an angry breath. "Even here, in my own kingdom, her influence has become insidious."

She attempted to push herself to sitting, her arms so weak they trembled. "Tell me what happens during the ceremony."

He sat gingerly on the bed, pressing her back down. "There are things we should not speak of outside of dreams."

Mireille's fingers found his forearm, bare below rolled-up sleeves. She tugged. "Come, then. Let us dream. "

Alder hesitated, but Mireille's heavy eyes were taking longer and longer blinks, and he finally lowered himself onto the bed beside her, letting her draw his arm around her as she shifted to her side, her breath uneasy and slow.

MIREILLE WOKE IN A MOONLIT GARDEN, fireflies dancing overhead, her unbound hair woven through tall grass and the scents of wisteria and honeysuckle all around her. She flexed her fingers, feeling well once more. She turned her face toward Alder who, inexplicably, lay on his side in the grass beside her.

Or not inexplicably, she supposed, because the dream was hers.

She ran a fingertip over the mark on his temple as his dark eyes traced the lines of her face. When she pressed up to sitting, he did as well. Her fingers entwined with his. "Tell me."

"When she attacks, I will be free to destroy her. I am more than an even match for her, but the bindings on my power must be broken." He drew his hand from hers. "But I cannot ask it of you. I will not risk your life further."

"I am at risk every moment. That risk is the very reason I am here."

"You came here for protection. I have nearly failed, time and again. If I fail once more, if you are harmed—" His words cut off, bitten back with something like rage and despair.

He would lose everything. His lands. His title. The bargain. Because he'd pinned all his hopes on Mireille. "I cannot break your bargain."

Alder went utterly still.

"I saw the enchanted hourglass. You needed her to believe that you loved me, and I you. You needed her to because you cannot marry for anything less." But he had no intention of falling for Mireille. He only meant to trick the queen.

His expression was a mask. "You saw the clock."

"The night of the ball. I was not certain of the details, but it felt of her magic. And there were hints, indications that you were bound by something more." What a fool she was to admit it, because he would know how she had discovered the truth. There was only one other person aware of the details, and that person was the queen.

"She got to you."

The words hurt, and more than they should. "She attempted to call it a ruse, certain that you could not be in love with me."

Alder was silent for a long while. He did not accuse her of betrayal, though surely the thought crossed his mind. He was clever enough to know what Maeve would offer. When he finally spoke, it was to say, "It seems she is no longer certain. She would not have risked coming for you again if she were." He looked at her, his gaze darkening with remembered anger, possibly of the real Mireille, feeble in his bed, barely able to sit up. "If you wish to continue, you will remain at my side. You will not be out of my sight again."

Something in her chest tightened. "And if I do not wish to continue?"

He looked away, brushing a shiny ladybird from his sleeve. "You have done everything I have asked. I will consider your promise fulfilled and your price paid. You will be free to go."

The queen would kill her in an instant without Alder. Norcliffe would be lost. And still... "You would truly set me free, when I am your only chance of beating her?"

His jaw shifted. "I can never truly beat her. She has removed any chance. My only hope was a default, to spur her into breaking our laws—had she openly and intentionally violated hospitality, I could move against her. But she has proved too canny to be baited into such a violation."

Mireille met his eyes, finding only truth in them. He would let his last opportunity slip through his fingers. He was trapped. He could not marry without love. It was the same as her friends in Westrende had always said, the price of breaking a bargain would be too dear to pay.

Mireille found, when she searched deep within her heart, that she did not truly have any other choice. She only hoped Norcliffe would survive her decision.

"We will go through with your plan."

CHAPTER 21

Mireille rested as the day wore into night. Thomas visited her, as did Kin and Noal—the latter of whom had taken the queen's act as a personal slight and was possibly plotting his own private revenge. Mireille made clear that she held no ill will toward the man, and that she herself had been under the queen's spell.

She did not admit it had happened in Alder's chamber.

The strength of the queen's influence continued to surprise them all, but they seemed more angered than unsettled, made worse by Maeve attempting to use the fae closest to Alder to see her work done.

Throughout Mireille's visits, Alder had stayed seated in a corner of the room, book in hand. His eyes remained on the page, but his fingers never lifted to turn one. Seeing her ready to drift off to sleep, Thomas had collected the playing cards he'd brought—a favored pastime of their youth—and had departed with a promise to remain only one room away. All had agreed that while Maeve was after Mireille, it would be unwise for Thomas to roam the palace on his own, so Kin had been assigned as his protector.

Alone again, eyes heavy, Mireille found her attention lingering on Alder. The sun dipped below the horizon, but he'd made clear she was not to leave his room. "Where will you sleep?"

His eyes did not leave the page. "I shall not."

"You should rest," he said.

Mireille wanted to argue, but the remedies continuously forced upon her had made her drowsy. Against her will, her eyes drifted closed, and sleep came swiftly.

Alder did not come to her dreams.

When she woke, morning light shone through the tall carved marble windows and he remained in his chair, though the book was no longer in his lap. He said, "Kin will draw you a bath, if you are ready."

She rubbed her puffy eyes but felt worlds better. "You trust me alone again?"

He stood. "No."

She gave him a look. He only approached the bed to offer his hand.

"I am steady," she promised, but took it nonetheless. Neither were wearing gloves, and the feeling of his bare skin on hers sent a jolt of awareness through her. He pulled her to her feet and she peered up at him, her thumb sliding across the back of his hand. "Thank you for watching over me."

"Perhaps you would have fared better as my prisoner after all. It seems I've done a poor job of it as your betrothed."

She asked, "Is it not bad luck for the groom to see the bride on their wedding day?"

"Only if the groom finds her displeasing." Then, seeming to realize what he'd said, his voice went gruff. "That is a human tradition."

Mireille suppressed a smile. "And what is fae tradition?"

Lifting her hand, he turned it, placing a light kiss on the center of her palm. "You will soon find out."

A jolt went through her, and she let out a shaky breath. Certainly, that had not been a show for the queen. Alder's eyes rose to hers. Her cheeks were hot, her pulse fluttering in her chest like a trapped bird.

There was a moment of stillness before his lips parted, as if to speak, and she wanted him to, desperately so. But a knock interrupted whatever he might have said. He released her hand, the door came open, and Kin stepped inside carrying a stack of towels. She glanced between them, then ducked her head, beginning to back away.

Alder cleared this throat, and Kin froze. "Please," he said. "Go ahead."

Kin crossed the room, head still dipped, then disappeared into an adjoining chamber. Alder gestured for Mireille to follow. She did, rather gratefully.

Mireille closed the door, bracing herself against it. The thrum of her heart was frantic, a rabbit's before prey. *Do you love him*, Kin had once asked. Fate help her, she did.

She was not certain what had happened, but she felt a bit betrayed. Her heart had always been strong. Sensible. Not a fool to chase a dream off a cliff.

There was only one thing she could do.

Straightening away from the wall, she signed to Kin, *I need your help*.

Kin's smile was warm and open; clearly the woman had no idea what a mess she might be taking on. She signed, *Anything*.

PLAN IN PLACE, Mireille had nearly steadied herself by the time she dressed and returned to Alder's company. He had not resumed his usual state, however, testing her lunch himself before she'd been allowed a single bite. As the minutes ticked by and the ceremony drew nearer, he grew even more cautious, and she was only permitted to return to her chambers to prepare with Kin, Nisha, and Thomas watching her every move.

Draped in the delicate wedding gown, Mireille did a slow turn before the mirror. Kin's anxious smile had Mireille wiping her palms. It would work. It had to.

She gave one final glance at her reflection, then nearly shrieked when Maeve's reflection peered back. It had been the queen's first opportunity to contact Mireille, and she had taken it. Behind her, Mireille could see Kin had noticed and, as she'd been warned, rushed to distract Nisha and the other fae ladies.

"Have you made your choice?"

Maeve's voice rang in Mireille's head, a knowing not unlike she had experienced in the dreams. Alder had been right, the connection felt stronger, and Mireille hoped she had not miscalculated her chances. The queen wore crimson once more, a celebration of her triumph.

But she had not won yet.

Mireille met her steely gaze. "I have."

"What is she on about?" Nisha said from across the room. Kin must have made a sign, because it was followed by an incredulous, "Practicing her speech? It is not a state dinner. She doesn't—what? Fine, yes, I'm listening. Stop grabbing at me like I'm a basket of scones."

Mireille leaned closer to the mirror. "He will escort me to the ceremony. I will announce to the entire court that we planned a ruse and our betrothal was never intended to go through."

Maeve's eyes lit with dark satisfaction. If Mireille would do such a thing, if she cared so little for Alder that she might humiliate him, then he would never go through with the ceremony, lest he forfeit his kingdom. "Of course it was a ruse," the queen purred.

"In exchange, you agree to never harm me, to leave my father, my kingdom, and the people of Norcliffe alone. You will bring no harm to those I love."

Maeve considered the words. It was asking a lot for a simple proclamation from Mireille, but the proclamation would mean Alder had lost his bargain with the queen. He must marry for love or Rivenwilde would be Maeve's. Mireille was willing to bet she wanted the fae lands more than she wanted Norcliffe. But lately, Mireille was betting on a great deal.

Maeve's lips curled. "It is a nice touch, announcing your ruse publicly. Adds to the disgrace. I like it."

"Well," Mireille said. "You know how I feel about fae who trap me in bargains."

Maeve laughed, the sound light and genuine. "To be sure." She lifted a hand, as if signing their contract in empty air. "Let our bargain be struck. You will make the agreed upon announcement, humiliate the prince, and I will leave your sad little kingdom and its people alone. *And* I vow to not so much as touch a single hair on your pretty little head, or anyone you truly love."

Heart thundering, Mireille could only nod. "I agree to your terms."

"What was that?" Nisha called from the connecting room, just as Maeve flashed a final wicked grin and disappeared from the glass. "Did you just say something about *terms?*"

Mireille turned to find Nisha striding back into the main chamber, Kin at her back, fingers twined anxiously together. Mireille gave the group a baffled smile, shoving her hands behind her back where a gold bracelet now hung at one wrist, its clasp heavy against her palm. "Are those not the ceremonial words?"

Nisha's gaze narrowed.

Mireille shrugged. "Well, it was certainly how Alder initiated our first bargain. Perhaps someone could let me know so that I won't do it wrong." She lifted the braceletless hand to tuck a lock of hair behind her ear.

Nisha did not seem convinced, but the room was empty of evil queens. Kin had fulfilled the favor Mireille had asked. All that was left, was for Mireille to pretend she was about to not get married.

CHAPTER 22

Mireille clung to Alder's arm as he escorted her down a torchlit path lined with flowering vines, moths fluttering near mounds of night-blooming honeysuckle, and blossoms trailing on a chill breeze. The sun was just beginning to set, casting everything it touched in an amber glow. A stole had been added to her dress for warmth, but she found being close to Alder's side was of much more comfort. It did not stop the anguish that twisted in her gut, but the look he had given her when he'd come to retrieve her had certainly helped.

Alder leaned near as a beautiful archway of orange blossoms came into view. They were being married in the lane. He had not told her.

His lips brushed her ear. "I will keep you safe, this time I swear it."

Mireille's chest swelled with warmth. And then, suddenly, a strange, fluttery panic. "Wait." She gripped his arm, and he stopped, turning to look at her. "I—" She could not tell him. She could say nothing she wanted to. She could only ask, "I must know. If this dress was truly my imagining, then how did it come to exist here, outside the dream, with every detail exact?"

"I remembered," he said simply.

"Every detail."

His brow pinched. "Of course."

Mireille drew a deep breath, then let it out with a shaky smile. "I am ready." She turned to face the path, arm in his.

He gave her a sidelong glance but continued on. As they reached the lane, the fae lining each side and dressed their finest turned their attention to the pair. Each held a tall taper, the flames defense against the dark.

Queen Maeve stood toward the end of the path in a place of honor as her station demanded, near a stone dais beneath the grandest orange tree of all. Delicate white blossoms draped low enough that they nearly brushed the dark hair of the fae officiant standing in wait.

Thomas stood near the front of the crowd with Kin by his side. Thomas was noticeably more anxious than Kin, which spoke volumes given that the fae woman knew a great deal more about what was to happen than him, but he gave Mireille a small nod.

Her chest squeezed. They were so very, very close to either victory or utter failure.

Soft music accompanied their walk, and as Alder and Mireille moved past the fae, their candles lifted skyward. Mireille was shocked to see her Westrende friends tucked into the crowd beside Nisha and her feral grin, and worried what bargain must have been struck to bring them there while securing both the fae kingdom's secrets and the safety of Westrende officials. She shot Alder an anxious glance. He whispered, "They were transported to the lane and shown nothing else. It seemed wise to permit them to witness our interaction with the queen, besides that Lord Holden demanded as much on your behalf."

It was not wise, but Alder had done it anyway. For her. She felt her mouth go soft and shaky.

"They are safe," he vowed. "No matter what."

She nodded, swallowing back what he evidently assumed was fear. He reached across his chest, squeezing Mireille's hand where it rested on his arm, then turned to face her before the dais. He took both of her hands in his. She could feel his magic, ancient and powerful, and truly could not believe what she was about to do.

As the officiant cleared his throat to speak, Alder tugged her a fraction closer, as if he could tell she might be about to do something rash—or, possibly, to bolt.

Voice low, she said, "You have asked me to trust you with much. I need you to trust me now, even more. At least for the next few minutes." She squeezed his hands then pulled free, and something that might have been fear flashed in his expression. Or, perhaps, he had been certain she would betray him all along.

Mireille stepped forward to address the crowd, trembling with nerves. The gathered fae stirred at the break in ritual, some appearing only intrigued while others seemed ready to act. She could feel the queen's magic, biting at her as if in anticipation, the bracelet's clasp hot on her wrist.

So much rode on this one thing. It had to work. She swallowed hard, curling the fingers of that hand into a fist.

"Regretfully, I must inform you all that this engagement has been a ruse." Gasps and excited murmurs broke out immediately, forcing Mireille to raise her voice. Evidence that at least part of those in attendance hadn't believed the ceremony would play through had her prickling in cold sweat. Pressing down the thought, she announced, "You have all been misled, and for that, I am sorry only that it may hurt those I truly love. The prince and I never intended to complete the ceremony."

Maeve grinned triumphantly from her spot beside the dais, as if the chaos of the crowd gave her strength, then the sharp sting of magic clawed up Mireille's body and down to her wrist.

The clasp snapped. The bracelet fell to the ground.

Mireille had done as the queen's terms had asked. The bargain had been sealed, as easily as that. Norcliffe and her father were safe, but only from direct attacks. And Mireille knew how those terms could be subverted, which meant they were not truly safe unless... Well, all that was left was to make Alder choose.

She turned to him, and the crowd hushed. His gaze lifted from the chain at her feet. There was something a bit feral in his expression, his posture seeming to want to act but unsure exactly what to do. He would not surrender, even when he believed all was lost.

Neither would she.

She stepped closer. "It was a ruse, a bargain, and you are the most brooding, confusing, and utterly vexing man I have ever known. All of those things are true."

The queen was gleeful, her magic dancing at Mireille's back, ready to devour all of Rivenwilde once the last sand dropped on her deal with Alder. Mireille did not spare her a glance. In fact, she was afraid her expression might give her away.

"Despite all of it, the danger, and the misery, and certainty that every day in this beautiful palace was wasted on me... for, you see, I understood that everything that mattered would soon be gone." She swallowed. "Despite all that, I fell in love."

Alder's jaw went slack. He looked for a moment as if unsure he'd heard her right, and then, all at once, like he had never quite seen her before. It pleased some deep part of Mireille that she had surprised him so thoroughly. And also, not a small amount, that he did not seem disappointed by her confession. The magic bit at her harder, painful fingers that wanted to lash at her.

She took another step toward him, her voice dropping. "I love you enough to break your curse, but only if at least some small part of you could love me in return."

He was silent for so long that Mireille worried she had judged the situation disastrously wrong. Perhaps his care and attention over her was truly only his vow, or that he merely needed her to draw the queen to the ceremony for his plans. Perhaps she would be the one to stand humiliated.

Perhaps she had cost them their chance at the queen.

She said weakly, "The curse surely does not require that you fall madly, head over heels. Even just a little bit, a small amount. If you loved me at all, it could work. We could be free of your bargain with the queen, before the last sands fall." Desperate, she pleaded, "I know that you need a princess of Westrende to break the Rive. I am sorry that I have kept—"

The bite to Mireille's skin went sharp, a rumble of power passed through the dais, and before she could get the words out, the queen laughed, loud and squawking, like carrion on a carcass, ready to claim her prey. It could be no accident the confession had been stopped. It was the single advantage Mireille had.

A pillar dropped to the earth. The queen stepped forward. "He will never marry you, fool. He would lose everything. Nothing matters more to the prince than this land. After all, it is all that he is." Maeve's voice dipped, and another pillar fell, crumbling before it even touched the ground. "He could *never* love you."

Mireille had lost her chance. The queen would act, and Alder would attack, and they would no longer be fighting bargains. They would be fighting the sands of time. She opened her mouth to shout the truth but before a word escaped, Maeve lifted her skirts to move, her magic rising through the space.

It was over.

Alder dropped to his knees.

"Mireille," he said, grasping both her hands in his. "I do. I do love you. Like a fool, for all of it—my kingdom, my title—I would give it up, if you would be my wife."

Behind them, Nisha let out a loud whistle, and at least one other fae in the crowd cheered. With the queen in attendance, it was an act of bravery, but very few understood what was truly at stake. It was not if Alder could find a true princess of Westrende on such short notice, if that was what he thought. He had assumed they had lost. And he was taking her as his bride on their way down.

He loved her. Genuinely. And they were nearly out of time to break the curse.

The queen surged forward, her fingers seeming too long for her hands. There was a darkness about her edges, and heat rolled off her, and though her voice turned cruel and hard, it somehow felt persuasive. "Adorable, truly. But, prince, she has betrayed you. She's all but admitted she's been in league with me this whole time." She held forward a hand and the chain lifted from the dais to settle in her palm. "We had a bargain, she and I. And look at you, down on your knees. *She vowed to betray you.*"

Alder stood, drawing Mireille near him as he stared at the queen. "I no longer care what you have to say. I will break our bargain, and the law will protect me. You intend to take Rivenwilde either way, but you cannot prevent our union."

A loud, harsh breath came out of the queen. Her arms had shifted wide, but Alder was right, she could not attack him or Mireille. They were all under bargain. And as for the people they cared about, well, the queen was a guest on Rivenwilde land. She was as bound as Alder.

He turned to the officiant, a tall man in ceremonial robes who did not appear in the least ruffled by the goings on. "Wed us."

The officiant nodded, placing one hand on his chest and raising the other where Alder and Mireille's were joined. The dais cracked in half.

"You cannot marry her!" Maeve screeched.

It was an actual, literal screech, and the entire crowd lurched backward.

Something changed in Alder's expression; he looked from Maeve to Mireille. She squeezed his hands tighter; there did not seem to be time to explain before the curse clock ran out, and Maeve had no intention of allowing Mireille to say it. Alder might not understand why the queen was so angry, but he was certainly clever enough to see that if that if she wanted to prevent the ceremony so badly, he should complete it, even if it only meant it might force her to act against him and break fae law.

He pulled Mireille against his chest, eyes on the queen, and ordered, "Do it."

The officiant began to speak but Maeve shrieked, "Cease, you fools!"

They did not cease. The ceremony carried on.

Maeve's chest heaved in a great wave.

Alder shoved Mireille behind him, commanding the officiant not to stop for anything.

With every word, Maeve breathed harder, until her body began to thrash. A screech tore through the air, and in the crowd several candles dropped to the ground, guttering out as fae scattered, some to safety, others to stand by their prince. Nisha herded Thomas and the other humans behind her, swords drawn, as Kin frantically signed toward the courtiers near the dais.

Noal calmly released the buttons of his coat.

Maeve's form warped and grew, twisting itself into a shadow creature like the one that had attacked at the sacred pond, but far, far worse. The remaining fae spread out into fighting stances while others watched from the shelter of the trees.

Mireille wasn't certain even the trees were safe. They swayed with the rumblings of magic, their tall trunks creaking and groaning in an unearthly way.

The creature that was Maeve stood twice as high as any in the crowd and knocked two of the largest fae near the dais aside with such force they landed in the distant shadows. The thing charged, and Alder moved for it.

Mireille had to stop him; they needed to finish the ceremony.

Too fast, the creature rose on its unfathomable haunches, long, knife-sharp talons bursting from its shadow hands. Alder's own hands drew back, but he was too close. The beast would tear him to shreds.

Mireille moved without thought, throwing herself between Maeve and the prince. A roar tore through the air, echoing off the trees bordering the lane. Shadowy claws rested a hair's breadth from Mireille's throat.

She stared up at the monster. "The laws of your land may allow you to act first, be punished later, but you and I have an agreement sealed by bargain. I have done exactly what you asked of me. You cannot harm me, nor can you harm my father, my kingdom, or the people of Norcliffe."

Mireille took hold of Alder's arm where he stood at her back, his chest rising and falling in angry, violent breaths. Her jaw tightened. "You may bring no harm to those I love. And I love the prince." She felt Alder melt against her, the way his body and his magic seemed purr in welcome and regard. He might believe his reign was about to come to an end, but it was clear he treasured the moment nonetheless.

He was barely touching her, but she had never felt more embraced.

Mireille vowed, "Soon, the Rive will come down, and Rivenwilde will ally itself with Norcliffe, and Westrende, and even the kingdom of Nordhelle."

The statement was not truly hers to make, but no one called her bluff, so she went on. "When the officiant finishes the binding and we are wed, what price must you pay to Alder?"

"Her lands will be forfeit," Nisha said from the steps of the dais. "They will belong to Alder, but Rivenwilde will remain severed due to the curse, so those lands cannot be joined with ours."

"She will be queen of nothing," Alder said with disgust. He slid a hand over Mireille's waist. "And it would be worth my crown to see that alone come to fruition."

Mireille felt sick. She'd seen how close the sands were to running out. She did not know how much longer the prince and Rivenwilde had left. It had truly been his last chance. The fae had not known the details of the curse, that the Rive would not fall unless he married someone of noble Westrende blood, only that if the Rive did not fall, Alder would never be king. Rivenwilde could never be free.

Nisha and several others stepped slowly closer, and the beast that was Maeve breathed its rattling breath.

Alder's grip drew Mireille against his chest. "So the question remains," he asked Maeve. "Why is it so important to that you prevent us from becoming wed, when to break fae law would cost you even more?"

A voice rose from the crowd. "I think I can answer that."

The creature whirled, baring its teeth and releasing a ragged snarl. Nisha flipped a sword forward, seemingly from thin air, and waggled it toward the beast. "It might not kill you, but it will certainly hurt."

Magic rose from the earth, stronger than Mireille had ever felt, shaking the entire platform and warming her to the core. "It might not kill you," Alder said. "But I am still Prince of Rivenwilde, and I will."

The creature's shadowy, malformed muzzle twitched, but it did not attack. Mireille wondered precisely how torturous being torn apart by fae magic was, given how even Maeve reacted to threat of it.

She tore her gaze away long enough to peer into the crowd, lit by flickering torchlight. The voice had come from the marshal of Westrende.

The marshal gave a little wave of acknowledgement. "You said he must marry a princess of Westrende."

"Yes," Mireille started. "He doesn't know."

"Ah," said the marshal.

Mireille turned to face her prince. "I hope you can forgive me. It was the only way we could think to keep me safe. You see, at first, we did not understand why a fae queen would be so set on ruining our kingdom, why she cared so much about the heir of a castle by the sea."

The creature gave a snarly little huff of air. Its skin was shifting into something like the bark of a hawthorn tree.

"The assault was relentless, and it cost—" Mireille swallowed hard. "It cost so much. When it became clear that her true target was me, Thomas and the others began an investigation. It seemed the queen had attacked neighboring kingdoms in recent years, all with one thing in common. But we had no way to defeat her. Clear was that she would not stop, even when Norcliffe was destroyed. So, we had to come. We had to find answers. We had to hope." She gave him her most earnest gaze. "My mother was not born in Norcliffe. She was from Westrende. A distant line, yes, but, well, there has been no one closer to throne for ages, given the misfortunes that have befallen nearly everyone of a royal line."

Alder's expression was one of true shock and, inexplicably, his gaze found the Westrende officials in the crowd.

"It's true," the marshal said. "You know they make officials study all the lineage and trade agreements. Perhaps I not as much as the magistrate here, but between us, we do have to have a thorough grasp of the law." The dark-haired man beside her stared on and the marshal said, "So that is your answer. The fae have kept a king from coming to power since long before Mireille's mother left for Norcliffe. She is the last Westrende princess, now that the others have been married off."

The prince stood in silence. The other humans present, representatives of Nordhelle and friends of the marshal, gave him a little wave.

The marshal crossed her arms, a bit smug that the prince hadn't sorted it all out. "Well, who's the clever one now?"

The blond-haired man beside the marshal tipped his chin toward the queen. "That's why she doesn't want you to go through with it. The wall will come down. The Rive will heal. She won't merely be the queen of nothing. You'll be the king of..." He gestured vaguely. "Everything."

The prince stared at the man, then the marshal, clearly in shock, but his hand did not loosen from around Mireille. His voice dripped with distrust. "And Westrende would allow that? You would cede its lands to me?"

The marshal's stance shifted, her hand resting on the hilt of her sword. "No." A breath came out of Alder, as if he had known it was too good to be true, but the marshal's gaze fell on Mireille. "We would cede it to her."

Thomas had clearly been able to get Mireille's message to Westrende—the favor she'd asked of him before—and though she had hoped their council would vote to support the union, and grant the marshal and magistrate leave to negotiate on their behalf, given that the Rive would fall regardless, it was in their best interest to have an ally in the fae and their new queen.

A noise came from Alder, seemingly rusty and disused, and Mireille glanced back to find that it was laughter. He had lifted his face to the canopy of sweet blossoms, letting the surprised, buoyant sound free. The crumbled pillars shook into dust as moonlight slid into the opening of the canopy, lighting the broken dais in a silvery blue glow.

Then his face turned down toward Mireille, still alight with a joy she could not truly believe, and he swung her around, arms locking her to him, and kissed her, long and deep. Beneath them, Rivenwilde sang, its magic humming through the earth and into every blossom and tree.

When the kiss finally broke, leaving Mireille breathless and wondering, the truth of their situation finally started to sink in. They were free. There were no more bargains, no more curses. Only her, and Alder, and safety for all their people.

On the dais behind them, Maeve had shifted back to her previous form, gown torn, crown askew. She was on her knees, no longer a queen, as the officiant had finished his declaration and the vows had been sealed with a kiss. Behind her, dagger in one hand, Noal reached forward and removed the woven crown with such satisfaction that Mireille had a sort of dastardly desire to watch him do it again.

The corner of his lips twitched, and he tossed the crown. Alder caught it with one hand, giving it a long, silent glance, before returning his gaze to Mireille. "Highness," he whispered, then placed the circle gently on her head, and leaned forward to kiss her again.

EPILOGUE

The prince had not agreed to allow the Westrende marshal and magistrate into the palace until Mireille threatened to offer both all the hospitality she might as queen of Rivenwilde. Because it was true, now that the curse was broken, the lands would be restored and Alder would be raised to his rightful place as king. He was the one who had married her after all, she reminded him.

Certainly, he could not have thought that she might suddenly grow meek.

The pair from Nordhelle, however, Alder treated with much greater courtesy and respect, which was to say, likely as much as he could offer a human—excluding Mireille, of course.

As her friends observed the interior of the palace awestricken, Mireille realized it had begun to feel comfortable and familiar to her. She briefly squeezed Thomas's hand, who had, of course, immediately forgiven her, even if he did seem slightly baffled and overwhelmed by the entire ordeal. Thomas had never been fond of ordeals.

They settled into a large sitting room, Alder, Mireille and her allies from Westrende and Nordhelle, who happened, happily, to be just as well-titled as she and legally able to negotiate on behalf of their kingdoms, plus Thomas, and Nisha. Noal and Kin stood to the side of the room, proprietary in their duties to their soon-to-be king and queen.

Mireille would need to write a letter to her father. The first of so, so many letters and documents to come.

The magistrate pointed to a line of text on a thick stack of contracts they had brought along and had been marking up for hours. "This section will outline the new border laws. Any fae bargains struck outside the of these marcations"—he gestured to a well-sketched map— "will be null and void."

"And your council will agree to this?" Alder's tone was once again that of a royal, sharp and dry and demanding respect.

He shot Mireille a look. "What are you grinning about?"

She only shook her head. It was not very queen-like to be giddy, to be sure. It would take all of them to restore their law, their lands, and bring down the wall without breaking something else. There was much work ahead.

The alliance was necessary, and there would be many compromises on both sides.

"And you truly will not allow the Rive to fall unless I sign this?" He lifted an eyebrow.

Mireille nodded curtly. "Truly." She loved him, but she would do what was necessary to protect their kingdoms. He was still fae, after all. It was not exactly a balance of power unless Mireille held her ground.

"Take her at her word, Alder," Nisha said from where she leaned against the wall, arms crossed. "My new sister knows how to get exactly what she wants."

Her eyes sparkled as she said it and Mireille gave her a

smile. Nisha's first act once she'd learned that the Rive would finally come down, was to announce her plan to roam the twelve kingdoms.

The pair from Nordhelle shared a private smile; Mireille didn't think she'd seen them stop holding hands.

The marshal said, "And of course we have stipulated the release of every single Westrende prisoner, with recompense."

"Oh," said Mireille. "I think I should tell you. I suspect the prince kept those royals and officers prisoner because the queen was going to…" She made a little neck slashing gesture.

The prince stared at her, as if mortally offended.

She said, "And from what Thomas and I saw, they were kept in reasonable comfort. I can't help but imagine it was an act of kindness, as terrible as that sounds." She smiled up at him. "Comfort is not the sort of thing one offers when merely attempting to thwart an enemy queen. He's really quite soft beneath that stern exterior."

He glanced at the marshal, then Noal, before his gaze went back to the contracts. "You have no proof of that." She thought she heard him mutter *ruthless* and *indefensible* under his breath.

"I believe the proof lies with the shadow creatures." Mireille leaned toward the marshal. "Do you know that the ones in Westrende are not Rivenwilde fae? Evidently, the queen had a legion of them, tied to her magic and her lands."

The marshal went still. "They were beholden to the queen? The ones that attacked Westrende?" Her focus narrowed on the prince, accusatory. "Not from Rivenwilde?"

"May we please get on with it?" he snapped. "I've had valets less difficult to negotiate with."

Noal took that moment to set a tray onto the table beside the prince. It held a silver dish loaded with sugarplums. "Majesty."

Nisha snorted a laugh.

The magistrate tapped another line in the contract, seemingly oblivious to the conversational diversion. "This will need signed by Mireille's father. Given that the king is well and there may be time for future heirs on Mireille's behalf—"

"All right. Enough."

The room went still at Alder's words, then he shifted, shoving the tray aside and dragging the last pages of the contract toward him. With a heavy sigh, he scanned through the details, lifted a quill, dipped it into an elaborately carved ink pot, then scrawled his name across the page.

Mireille's chest felt as if a flock of birds might burst free. The queen was defeated. Norcliffe was safe. And she... She was in love with her prince.

She looked to Thomas, and he offered her the steadiest of grins. He had, of course, agreed to remain in Rivenwilde as her advisor. He still wore the fine suit tailored for the wedding, but now there was a ribbon tied around his wrist, in exact same shade as Kin's dress. Mireille took in the woman and the other occupants of the room, finding that, though she was eager to visit her father and her kingdom, she had already found a new home. And even though it might prove daunting, for the first time in a long while, she wasn't scared at all.

"Noal," the prince said. "Show these guests to the," he made a shooing gesture, "somewhere with some sort of refreshments." He turned toward Mireille, his hand finding hers as if he'd done it a thousand times. "I have a desire to take to the gardens with my wife."

As the others ambled from the room, Mireille turned to face him. "The gardens?"

He made a short, satisfied sort of hum.

"It is nearly sunrise. Are we to visit the wisteria tree?" She laid a hand on his chest. "I find I've grown quite fond of Rivenwilde and its heart."

He placed his hand over hers, expression solemn, and

Mireille could feel his magic in a way she had not before. Soon, the land would heal, he would take his throne, and that power would increase by untold measures. He said, "Majesty, the heart of Rivenwilde now beats for you."

"Truly," she whispered. "I could ask for nothing more." And then she kissed him.

Reign of Shadows

SHATTERED REALMS

King of Ash and Bone

Queen of Iron and Blood

- WITCHY PNR -

HAVENWOOD FALLS

Toil and Trouble

BAD MEDICINE

Blood & Brute & Ginger Root

Visit the author on the web at

www.melissa-wright.com